Mogue Doyle has been in the building trade most of his life. He and his family live in County Wexford, Ireland. His first novel, *Dancing with Minnie the Twig*, is also published by Black Swan.

Acclaim for *Dancing with Minnie the Twig*:

'A terrific first novel: fresh, sparky, yet deeply felt'
Edna O'Brien

'I was swept along with the characters throughout the novel . . . contains wonderful natural language, and it positively drips with imagery. I became so caught up in the flow of the writing, that it was hard to stop and think just what it was that made the novel so good. Doyle's characters ring true, and they all experience conflict . . . Doyle's descriptive language is wonderful . . . The novel is wonderfully structured too. Doyle has bucket loads of talent. Not only do I agree with Edna O'Brien, I don't think she was being enthusiastic enough. I simply adored this evocative book'
Books Ireland

'A lyrical account of childhood, told through the eyes of a boy who is confused and disenchanted in the changing Ireland of the 1950s and '60s . . . reminiscent of Pat McCabe's *The Butcher Boy*'
Ireland on Sunday

'An evocative tragi-comedy with a poignant twist in its tail'
Woman & Home

'A glorious evocation of rural Ireland in the 1960s, a sad and funny account of a young boy growing up in the country; and written in language that is idiomatic and lyrical . . . rich in imagery'
Irish Post

'One of the simplest, and blackest rites of passage books you will come across from rural Ireland'
In Dublin

'A début novel that opens with the narrator attending his own funeral, then goes on to explain the events surrounding the funeral in counterpoint to the events which led to the funeral, then drops clues along the way as to how the narrator finished up in the hearse, and is still able to hold the reader to the final page is a promising début by any standard . . . keeps the reader hooked'
Sunday Tribune

Also by Mogue Doyle

DANCING WITH MINNIE THE TWIG

and published by Black Swan

A MOTH
AT THE GLASS

Mogue Doyle

WITHDRAWN

BLACK SWAN

A MOTH AT THE GLASS
A BLACK SWAN BOOK: 0 552 99986 5

Originally published in Great Britain by Bantam Press,
a division of Transworld Publishers

PRINTING HISTORY
Bantam Press edition published 2004
Black Swan edition published 2005

1 3 5 7 9 10 8 6 4 2

Set in 11/14pt Melior by
Falcon Oast Graphic Art Ltd.

Black Swan Books are published by Transworld Publishers,
61–63 Uxbridge Road, London W5 5SA,
a division of The Random House Group Ltd,
in Australia by Random House Australia (Pty) Ltd,
20 Alfred Street, Milsons Point, Sydney, NSW 2061, Australia,
in New Zealand by Random House New Zealand Ltd,
18 Poland Road, Glenfield, Auckland 10, New Zealand
and in South Africa by Random House (Pty) Ltd,
Endulini, 5a Jubilee Road, Parktown 2193, South Africa.

Printed and bound in Great Britain by
Cox & Wyman Ltd, Reading, Berkshire.

Papers used by Transworld Publishers are natural, recyclable
products made from wood grown in sustainable forests. The
manufacturing processes conform to the environmental
regulations of the country of origin.

For Mary, for all her support.
For Páidín, for his fund of knowledge.

ONE

1960

There was a time, and a right good time it was, when I loved the black of night and thought that everything about evenings was magical. As soon as twilight's dark pollen dusted out the last of a day's light, all tiredness would lift and a fresh vigour flow through my veins.

Badgers, foxes and old owls went on the prowl the one hour as I'd begin my wanderings. They were, in a way, my accomplices; we had something of the same hunting instinct, a feel for the kill. From the stage of evening that the blue-black of the Blackstairs mountain would rise to cover the blood-red of the sun, eventually blotting it out completely, my expectations for the night ahead would likewise rise and quickly soar to match the height of the mountain.

Yes, night in this neck of the woods always began

with a blue-black patch in the middle of the Blackstairs, then rose like dark dust spores, spread itself over the countryside and settled thickly down here along the valley. The bright enamel of the sky would give way to light charcoal, and one deeper shade gradually overlay another till all was pure black.

The thing about the night was how alive you'd feel; the body's senses on high alert, searching out what was close by. Who's that walking the road ahead? The sound of the voice, or that particular footfall, would be the giveaway. The scent from a room, too, before you'd even touch the door handle, would let you know that a certain lady was in there – ah, sweet expectation!

In those early days, thirty-three years ago, it was the sense of touch that gave most pleasure. The accidental brush against a sprouting, maybe even a full, bosom, a nudge of knees with the person sitting alongside and that touch of fingers on the dance floor all spoke loudly, promised so much. The memory of those moments – by heavens, their very warmth yet – is almost enough to remove the chill from this night. For cold it is that's all about nowadays.

To be honest – if such a thing is possible – what I liked most about the dark was the absolute freedom, the freedom most undercover creatures have, to take part in the wild goings-on of night. To pull the door behind you on leaving the house, down the lane and out onto the open road under cover of darkness; it was possible to turn right or left, go up or down the road, without prying eyes wanting to know your business or keep you under heel. It was helpful, too, when calling to a neighbour's house, to know who was inside ahead of you; so I'd tell myself to have a little look in the window first, and then decide whether to go in or not – and what harm is there in being careful, before you jump to conclusions? Indeed, the dark was a young man's best friend when it came to dealings with the ladies. Ah, the ladies . . . but we'll keep that for later.

I wish it were otherwise, but certain things can't be changed. It just wasn't my lot to become a butterfly under the warm summer's sun and flit from one flower head to the next, but instead to flutter like mad: a moth against the window pane, hell-bent on reaching the flame of some half-light inside. The fact is I was a creature of the night; still am.

I know this road like the back of my hand. From the end of our lane, I can make out every rough stony patch of ground, every last briar sticking out to tear at my trouser legs. And here we are: this place up ahead, the farmyard on the right. Slow down now and listen: the initial check. There's a dim glow at low level across the road, a patch of borrowed light from the yard inside.

I ought to have the picture in my head by now: after all my winters of coming, unseen, to this place to watch her. Wonder if she's wearing that blue bib, the one with red flowers and a red border, that tightens so severely about her body – still curved, firm after all the years. With a scarf to cover her hair, her head is tucked in against the cow's big right flank, pushing the animal's weight onto its other hind leg to make room for her to squeeze away on the teats. The cow tugs on the neck-chain, screws back its great head to smell and eye her up – make sure it's Kate – before consenting to take part in this rite. The moment that happens, she reassures the animal: Yes, Betsy, it's only me; over onto your other leg now, good girl. The familiarity of the voice eases the tension in the dumb beast's frame, and the bulbous eye softens.

I feel my way off the stones of the cowhouse gable: hard as flint, cold to the touch. Over to the corner granite with that sharp-cut edge; never lost its shape either. Turn right, stay in by the wall, and up to the door. It's open; January or June that door is open. Must mind now not to step into the light – still not used to all this electricity business: such sudden brightness at only the flick of a switch, since we got connected up three years ago. There's the spatter of milk now: it's safe to move further.

And there's Kate. The pale flesh on this side of her face, the flushed red on the back of the left hand and the curved calf of her left leg. Such lines, colour! Look at the way she sits, tilted forward on that three-legged stooleen, so absorbed with what she's doing. She has the knack of applying herself totally, and with such ease, to the work in hand; just like her brother. The powers of concentration that that fellow had! No, mustn't think of her brother. There's already enough going on in my head.

It's a craze that has me driven demented. The craving to be close to what was, a long time ago, the centre of my world and the main house-of-call for many local people. There's this queer sort of hope that, through some miracle, time will change and I'll get back to that fatal year to undo what happened. There's a yearning to retrieve lost days, and nights, of unending excitement, the whirlpool of *craic* . . . and music. Yes, the music: that one tune, St Anne's Reel, forever going round in my head. I can't reason away the impulse to be at this door – this entrance to the world of the bygone. And the more time passes, the stronger it gets, the more urgency there is to do something about the craving; possibly even take that gigantic step into the light – no, not this accursed cold electric light, but the other brightness: the one we had before.

I remember those nights of half-light. Paraffin lanterns and tilley lamps outside; inside, black oil lamps on nails in walls, with trout-brown smoked-up globes. A time when the silver Aladdin and its cone-shaped filament glowed on the oval table in the middle of the parlour floor. And because of it, the damask linen tablecloth had changed from white to yellow clay. Flickering candles would sway the shapes on the whitewash – turned sepia – and there were shadows everywhere, and that tune played on . . .

Stolen kisses in the porch while passing in or out, and awkward touches not so instantly repelled there in corners of lesser light and behind doors. The half-whispered *Will you meet me outside later?* plea, and that longed-for *Yes* following a moment's wait, the scarcely bearable moment's wait. And later, outside, shadows would merge along the ground or arms reach out to be clasped: couples on their way to the haggard to take the longings off each other. The haggard – the large area of yard beyond the main yard that only ever came into its own during the harvest and, of course, at night. And the dwelling-house over there at the top of the yard was then a half-lit trout pool teeming with young life, in those years before nineteen twenty-seven.

She ought to be finished by now, surely. I'll move back into the yard – careful where you put your feet: there's a lot more puddles than there used to be. Ah, the light's on in the kitchen, while the cowhouse and dairy below have turned to darkness. So many lights, so much bloody brightness, ever since the Scheme came round. The yard lamp, though, is the one to mind; I nearly got caught out, once or twice, before getting the hang of things. Its switch is inside the porch. Must get over to the kitchen window and watch out for her opening the porch door, and be ready to scamper off.

It's all right: she's sitting by the fire, where her mother used to sit, turning the fanners. She has the kettle down on the lowest notch of the crane, boiling water for the tea. It never changes, this nightly routine. Having let the tea draw for an exact five minutes in the hot *greesach* of the hearth, she carries the enamel teapot over to the table and sits in. Soda bread is buttered with a bone-handle table knife on a blue-rimmed plate, which she then smears lightly with a coating of blackcurrant jam; all her own produce, 'cept the tea.

The time of the Emergency made her that way, made everybody like that: all the coupons and rationing. But afterwards, she stayed spartan, while everyone else went back to the ways of plenty. And you could set your watch by her; you'd think she was a Protestant. The one luxury, if you can call it that, is the shocking-red leather car seat raised off the ground on a timber frame over by the fanners. It's not that it's grotesque or anything like, but, among the other, more severe, simple pieces of furniture, is there not a certain out-of-place look to this one fad that, maybe, borders on bad taste? I just don't like the lurid thing.

After supper she turns on the wireless for the half-six news and Michael Dillon for the cattle prices; then switches it off. Kate will sit there in silence looking into the fire till bedtime – of a Wednesday night, she won't go to bed till after *Farmers' Forum* ends at ten o'clock. This is our spell, when she and I can think about the same things – though I never think of anything else. Kate beside the warm crackle of burning logs inside, and I out here on the sill – in the less warm night air, I can tell you. It's our dream time . . .

Shhh, there it is. Listen now, can you hear it rising: that tune? The reel, St Anne's Reel. And there he is coming into focus at the table, the same table; smiling, I'm sure – forever damned-well smiling – playing the box. Oh no, excuse me, not playing it, he never actually played the cursed thing; the fellow just flitted his hands effortlessly up and down the keys of that old Hohner; the long bony fingers only talked to one another through sounds the buttons made. Philly's eyes, black holes for eyes, look out at me from beyond the empty space, and are gone.

Philly Kelly's shape it is, right enough, at the corner of the table. His laughing face and freckled cheeks are just like his sister's, but unlike his sister he has jet-black curly hair, straight off some old Greek statue. His tall, lean-as-ever frame bends over the box to listen to its sounds, and tells it to make clarion notes this way or that. The way old Jigger Nowlan used to shape iron on the horn of an anvil: the same immaculate control working with a purpose.

I know the purpose: he's calling the others, through the second part of that tune. The reveille goes out to all who came to this place back in those heady days – nights, I mean nights. And they respond. Time for an old session.

Here they are on cue out from the shadows, blustering onto the floor; their feet flicker up and down to the reel. There's the full foregathering of them now. The steel toe and heel tips as piercing as soldiers' bayonets, thanks to Jim the Shoe or Mylie Fitz – each as good a cobbler as the other: one-and-a-half pairs of working boots a day, finished. The best, oh, only the very best, will do for such company. They move onto the centre flag, the special one – spot the change of sound when you listen closely: something of the timbre of a bass drum to it, Philly used to say, with the beat of a heart. And no wonder.

It's only like yesterday, that Philly and I went to Glasslacken Quarry for that flagstone. We spent hours mulling through stockpiles of uncut slate in the sludge and muck of a mid-February to select the right shape, one big enough to take a dance set. That section of quarry where the flags had been stacked in groups, a dozen per group standing on their edges and leaning against each other like dominoes, seemed our best bet.

This one here doesn't look too bad, says I, having turned over at least twenty of them heavy shaggers. Philly strolled over, looked at it sideways, with one eye closed, and ran the palm of his hand round the nape of his neck. The exactness with which his brain clicked hadn't changed one iota since our schooldays, when we'd been the best of friends.

I don't like the way the grain tapers off, says he. It might split. He was right of course; the trouncing that stone would get, it wouldn't last. A carpenter like myself, used to the grain-runs of wood, should have seen that flaw. Philly, used only to drill-runs and hobbing-off horses along them, had spotted it. My enthusiasm for the venture slipped; he could pick his own blasted stone. My job was no more than to lay it in place; what I'd agreed to do when asked. An hour passed before he settled on one, and even then he wasn't quite satisfied – all bloody perfectionists are the same; they'd get to you. Or was he dallying on purpose, just to show what a big fellow he was?

Back here afterwards, I lifted some small flags from the middle of the kitchen floor and scooped out a hole to an exact depth. It was Philly's notion that a horse's skull be laid in the hole, and propped so that the bone would touch the underside of the new flag in a certain way. I layered small stones around the edges, and a coating of sand over; then with a few last, levelling adjustments the flagstone was set in place. Be the hokey, it's there yet, look.

The reverence at the final act was like that shown for baptism in church. Philly called Kate, pointed her onto the new stone and lilted a hornpipe. He stopped after a few bars, but Kate kept dancing in time to some music beyond hearing. She sure could move. So caught up was I with the sound of her foot-tap that what should've been relished wasn't: her ease of movement, the sight of an ankle and the graceful curves of high-flying legs. But that didn't stop those shapes before me from being implanted in my head, like marks on stone from a mason's cold chisel.

Then Philly joined in, easily merging with his sister's step. 'Cept, to protect his bandaged right arm, he danced but lightly. It was obvious that the sound was . . . well, different. Not sure, I searched his face for a sign, but none was given. When they finished, it was exactly on the beat together, as if they'd spoken to each other in the secret language that only music people understand. You'd feel out of place with them.

That'll do, says he then. The horse's head underneath is the thing all right. He didn't look at anybody while saying it, or afterwards; he didn't need anyone else's nod. Once Philly said the sound was right, well, there could be no more about it. His verdict was what mattered, the ultimate stamp of approval. And wasn't it well he knew it too, as he strutted out of the kitchen? You'd think nobody else had an ear or taste in such matters.

What was all the fuss about anyway? A special bloody flagstone, a hole dug out and the horse's head stuck down, to get a little more clickety-clack during a dance. Or was there more to it than sound? Some ancient rite, maybe, that Philly was once again carrying out. You'd wonder what went on inside that fellow's head. Could it have been he was part of some old pagan sect who'd had their beginnings way back in the mists of time, long and ever before religions were heard tell of?

There'd always been something to Philly that I couldn't quite put my finger on, and this was it. Pishoguery. He was in league with the other world, the fairies. You'd see it in the small things, the little observances he'd keep. Saw it for myself like: the way he'd lift a finger to his forehead in salute of a magpie, and he'd hesitate for an instant passing the well-field gate, as though paying his respects to some unseen thing there under the old whitethorn. And the way a bush was put up every year for Beltane: the end of it stuck down in the dunghill at the bottom of Kellys' yard. The bits of rag and eggshells hanging from its stark twigs would blow and rattle at every puff of wind of early summer.

18

You'd know it was Philly who'd put the thing there. Hard to believe it, like, from a grown man.

The trouble there was over that, though. At least we hadn't seen much wrong with cutting the head off Doran's dun cob – and such an amount of blood. Had I planned it better, I'd have made a cleaner job of it, less gory. In a way, I was doing the animal a favour by putting it out of its misery. It was nearing its day for the knacker's yard anyway, and old Doran had stopped working it long and ever before. By sacrificing itself to us in this way – though it hardly had much choice in the matter – it would become part of something big, with a more important role to play than any it'd ever had, and with a lot more lasting to its new existence. A dance was planned for after the District Final, and win, lose or draw that match, Philly had said, our hurling team's achievements were going to be celebrated. The dance must go on.

The horse's head was boiled in a potato pot – see that big iron one in the corner opposite Kate, there against the hob. Slow-boiled it, we did, for a few hours, the same as you'd do a bouillon, so as not to damage the bone, if you don't mind; then picked off the flesh and cleaned out the innards. Would you like a taste? says Philly. Yuck! He ate a piece of flesh himself – again doing the big fellow on it, or was there something more grisly in his action? We spent surely a full day between going to the quarry, cooking the head and laying that stone in place.

Old Doran kicked up a fuss and went to the Guards. Don't know what he expected them to do. The long fellow, Guard Ryan, did go round on his bike all right, asking questions of anyone he met; that was his duty. Might you have any information now about the killing of Mr Doran's horse? says he, waiting to pounce with a pencil stub and black book on any scrap of information. But he got nowhere with his enquiries: people round here gave him short shrift.

There was no love lost on fellows in uniforms. Soldiers, RIC, Tans and the Free State Regulars had previously travelled these same roads, imposing themselves. Then another set appeared: the Civic Guards. All the bloody same. The Troubles might have been over, but people hadn't forgotten, least not for long enough to allow them to separate the new lot – supposed to be our own – from the old RIC. A question of trust, really: put a uniform on your best friend, and even he'd turn into a minion to make notes about you. Police, officials and informers, all that ilk – always prying – are best avoided.

No, nobody talked, only among themselves – and they certainly knew how to do that. Oh, I hear Old Doran has a search party out for the head of his horse, says Ben Rowe. The man wants to sew the missing part back on, and sell it the next time there's a circus in town. It should make a good fist of dancing a hornpipe.

Everyone knows every blasted thing, I says. Can a body do one thing without half the country hearing about it?

'Cept for the Peelers and old Doran, says he.

Aye, I hope he finds his head, says I, cutting short the conversation.

Big Cha Cha Tobin, too, made the most of the caper. He asked Philly if he'd heard the latest ghost story. The one about the Headless Horseman, says he.

I did, says Philly, and so did the rest of the parish.

But now, says Cha, there's another version to that story.

Is there indeed? Philly's wry smile showed that he'd expected a smart quip, but wouldn't gratify Cha by asking him what it was.

Cha waited to be asked. But without the impact he'd hoped for, he eventually says: He carries his head round under his arm for safety sake, in case anyone might want to cut it off. Do you get it? says he. Cut it off . . . the head?

Philly laughed all right, not at the joke but at the slow, low voice of Cha; the meek way Cha had muttered it with his lips curled down at the edges like a sad clown. For the same Cha Cha Tobin was really no more than a big clown, an interfering lug of a clown.

Nobody had talked. And the fact that my brother, Mylie, had let it be known that he'd held on to his rifle since the '23 ceasefire – didn't bury it, like what others had done, in a boghole to rust – was a deterrent to any would-be informer. There's always one shagger in the woodpile who needs reminding, says he. People respected the likes of Mylie, who were known to have held on to their pieces.

Oh, Guard Ryan knew all right who'd done it. Three and four times on his rounds, he quizzed me and Philly with the same questions, letting on to have forgotten our answers while fumbling with the notebook on the handlebars of his bike. He looked me up and down a bit too suspiciously: I was tempted to floor him. I'd let him see quickly enough that there was another rule in these parts, a different sway to his kind. An independent people were rooted on these slopes, who'd always be here. I had a surge of what Mylie must have felt when he was on the run: a loathing for bullies in uniforms who called their business *official* and were convinced of their natural right to step on everyone else's toes. This instinctive, yet cold, hatred rose through me: could have done for him on the spot. But Ryan read well, I had to grant him that: he knew better than to press too hard with his questions. It wasn't the first time we'd crossed paths. With one last look at me, he closed the black book, threw a leg over the bike and pushed away up the road.

* * *

Cha Cha and Philly, along with their old spectre friends, all fade back now among the shadows, and the floor is empty again. The music, too, slips from my head. I feel the chill; can't resist it penetrating my bones the way I used to. And the window sill is beginning to freeze over. This old army coat of mine is gone too threadbare — come the next fair of Borris and I'll get myself another good one; though they don't have the quality things there any more either. Nothing is the same any more.

Nothing is the same except the hauntings of spectres, and their tormenting my head. Life wasn't as difficult to put up with, in the early days that followed the event: there were so many other things to be concerned about. But as time passed, the haunting increased, and now almost all waking hours are taken over by it. Something will have to be done; this obsession can't go on.

But as far as this night goes, Kate can sit there on her own by the fire till bedtime. I'm going to take this bag of bones on home before the *kinleen-roes* start growing from my nostrils. An army coat calls for a soldier-like march. Left right, left right . . . but must be careful till I get out onto the road. Down the road, up the lane into my own small yard and I'll lift the latch on the door of my cottage.

Aye, and I'll find what's sitting there inside, waiting for me . . .

TWO

She's always there like a broody hen – a great fluffy
Rhode Island Red – when I get home. On a low stool
at the other side of the fire, staring into the *greesach*,
she rarely lifts her eyes. You'd wonder what she
sees in that fire. The changing shapes of the coal
embers that glow and fade, as puffs of air move
across their surfaces, catch her eye and remind her
of other shapes, other times, maybe.

   The terrier under the table recognizes me when I
go through the porch: he lifts his head and, by way
of a stump-tail stirring, says hello. Looks at me
with large tender eyes that remind me of what her
eyes were like, with a certain clear sparkle, before
their colour became somehow dissolved. Any
minute now – aye, when ready – he'll come over,
jump up and scratch my shins with his two front
paws.

24

Your supper is on the table, is all she says, without lifting her head.

A plug of smoky bacon, cold and fat, turning a shiny puce on a saucer covered by another saucer slipping off, is there the two days since Sunday's dinner. On lifting the top saucer, I get a whiff – scarcely appetizing. Anyway, the dog won't go hungry tonight. As I butter a piece of bread, my carpenter's hands, with their lines like slits, feel bulky round the steel-handle knife, and I'm reminded of Katie doing the exact same thing earlier; except she used the knife with delicate ease. As if by its own accord, my black thumbnail slides beneath one of the many slits in the oilcloth table cover that's seen better days – there these twenty years, it was once a bright yellow. I lift the edge and let it drop, again and again; faster till it becomes a clicking rhythm. The cricket-like noise breaks the quiet, but I wonder will she notice.

The dog crawls back under the table, and when my boot drops on his haunch – of course, it's by accident – he yelps more from start than pain. At last she lifts her eyes from the fire, and her body shows some movement; but only to put her hand on the fanners to wind the wheel. With the door and windows shut, a smoke that'd cut the eyes out of hell's demons will soon rise. Smokehouse smoky bacon, smokescreen and signals. And smoke in my eyes.

*　*　*

I should've stayed at home tonight; wasn't quite in form for traipsing up that hill to sit on a freezing window sill. The chill hasn't left my bones yet. To climb under the blankets upstairs is what I look forward to, with the light off and the world shut out. There's a yen to escape, and take myself back in time. But it's from the warmth of my bed that I'll face all the spooks for the rest of this night. Would that, for once, they'd not come. Though what would we do without each other, me and my spooks?

This last step of the stairs creaks worse than the others; it ought to've been repaired ages ago. Is there not a carpenter left in the country – apart from this one? But what tradesman puts right his own house while there's another one elsewhere to be fixed? Except for my father before me; now there was a great man for keeping things right. My mother wanted for nothing while he was alive. A mason by trade, he could turn his hand to anything – till he up and died when I was ten. Consumption, they said he had – aye, and not the only one, either, of my crowd that it took. I've forgotten even what he looked like. It's as if he never was.

Yet he dwelt in this house, slept in this room, himself and my mother, for part of my lifetime. And my father walked these hilly roads, knew every bend along the crooked lanes of Springmount, and every other townland round here besides; knew them better than most people. It was said: only the sheep-men, who live farther up, whose herds roam the commons to the top, saw the mountain as often as he did. Every Sunday after first Mass, he would take off with a pack of dogs to hunt rabbits across the hills, and not come back till night.

He'd've been aware of how the mountain changes her coat through the seasons. Especially her colour. The fullness of yellow furze everywhere: from fresh daffodil-like tint in spring to the golden bloom of high summer. Then a new coat for the autumn lady: browns and purples throughout to match the sloe-purple of the rocks above. He'd've watched in awe as a late afternoon sun broke through the clouds in great heavenly rays, like in a holy picture, to expose those hidden valleys across the hillside and brighten up stretches of fields into vibrant green patches. One part of a field might be full of light and the other part in shade, the rain teeming down. Sometimes I think his ghost is to be seen through the moods of the Blackstairs. It's the only hope I've got left of knowing him.

I look out, too, for bends on lanes, knobs of old furze bushes and places roundabout that in the meantime haven't changed. They might hold something of his essence, left there as he dallied for a moment. The older I get, the more I try to picture his face. But in vain. He's covered his tracks too well, the man.

Anyway, we could do with him around this house now, if only to make a few repairs. Aye, so many items need fixing, but they'll stay as they are and see me out. Leave them to the next man. I have other things on my mind.

After ages of tossing and turning, searching the dark corners of the room, my ghosts are still nowise to be found. The only distraction was when she – always see her as that, *she*, have done so for years – came up the stairs. I thought of her there on the last step, creaking it like some odd alarm clock, and pictured her passing my door, into the other room and across the boards. Would she let anything fall on the floor tonight – accidentally, of course? Five more minutes before the bed would start to creak. Then the quiet.

Separate beds in separate rooms, never a hint of change – too late for that now. It's how it's been since shortly after I first brought her here. Ah, wasn't she the beauty then: those eyes, the jet-black hair! But old gripes, often as small as makes no odds, somehow grow, like toadstools overnight, so enormous between people as to prevent recall of how they ever came about. A monument to detachment, maybe. Of course, then, I would stray in there from time to time: more out of necessity than longing. And always in the dark – easier that way: no expressions or eye catching eye. Fair play to her, though, she seldom rebuffed me. But those forays didn't last.

Her nightly sobbing in the early years always woke me – the times I'd have been asleep anyway – and it wasn't easy to resist the urge to go in and comfort her. Had that happened, maybe the ice would have thawed rather than thickened, and we might've become good friends. But that mixture in my head, of numbness one minute and turmoil the next, had already taken hold. And a prisoner in stocks and chains is hardly much use to a crying, wanting woman.

I knew there was something I couldn't quite bring to mind till now – the idea of crying, I suppose, reminded me. She has been reading that letter again, the one from Simon. With the usual last glance round, on the first step of the stairs, I noticed the corner of the envelope sticking out of her bib pocket. She'd probably spent half the day crying into it, but would she want me to know that?

You'd find things out for yourself though; given time, you'd sense what's in people's heads. Anyway, don't secrets have a habit of poking their little heads from even the darkest niche? Oh, I got to read it all right, in spite of all her minding. How'd I manage that? Just bided my time, that's all. As she is with everything, it was bound to be only a matter of days before she'd get heedless. And on Sunday morning last, I found it in the pocket of her bib; she'd forgotten to transfer it to her handbag going to Mass.

The writing certainly didn't change my impression of him. The small letters barely legible, the long narrow 'h's and 'l's and the lines sloping up towards the right: a sure sign of meanness. Who did he take after that way? He talked of little else in the letter but himself, the wife, two children (who've never as much as laid eyes on their grandparents), his house and the life he has. At the very end he remarked: Hope this letter finds you well, and P.S. I don't suppose the old chappie has popped his clogs yet . . . I had to stop reading, though there was another line or two to go, and I put the thing back in her bib. It was like a hand had reached up from the page to grab at my throat, and the contempt in that half-cockney accent.

He's been over there for the last fifteen years, since he was eighteen in 1945, and you'd count on two hands the number of times he's written home. A fortune would be made, he'd believed, rebuilding London, and when the war was over he took off from here. He was gone before I knew it. Where was Simon last night? I says to her the next morning, seeing that his bed hadn't been slept in. He'd been in my room since he was a toddler, nearly. I wasn't told anything about that move either, not a word in advance; only to find his bed in the corner when I opened the door one night, and a bundle lying there curled up asleep.

Was I annoyed that he'd parked himself in my room? Not in the slightest; glad really, to see that he was at the age of cutting his apron-strings. His presence there, though fast asleep, became a comfort to me: it took some of the sting from the stillness of the room. The arrangement brought about a certain companionship – if you could call it that, exactly – between father and son that she had, up to then, done her best to prevent. Too much old mother's mollycoddling never did a young fellow any good. And so many things I could've taught him: to go hand-poaching brown trout in the mill race, or shape a hurl with a plane and spokeshave. So many places we could've cycled to of a Sunday afternoon: the hurling matches – who knows, maybe he had the makings of a hurler in him – or hunting with dogs over the mountain.

He went away, says she, not very forthcoming with the details.

Away where?

Where do you think?

If I knew, why would I be asking?

Over to London. Hasn't he been saying it for ages? Don't tell me you didn't know.

There was a familiar irritation in her voice, and I didn't fancy watching it grow: the opening up of old sores, or that endless sobbing of her earlier years. While it's doubtful the situation would've got so out of hand, I still didn't want to risk it.

That's all was ever said between us on the matter. His going away without telling me was just another betrayal: that old knife-in-the-back feeling from an earlier time. But could you say such a thing? Huh! Disloyalty was all around, but its effects . . . Well, you had to just grin and bear them.

He landed home in a flash suit the following August, and not a word out of him could you understand – cor blimey this, cor blimey that. And all the *geezers* he'd run into down the tube station. He wasn't back here three days when Shem Brien, the postman, had a letter for him. Afterwards, Shem spotted me working on a roof, got off his bike and shouted up: *Oi mite, ove you been ouver? Ove you 'ad a billet-doux from your bourd lately?* Shem could take people off all right, and had the accent spot on. Anyway, he'd have heard it often enough: most of his youngsters had gone to England.

Well now, Simon must've found a *bourd* for himself, and, regular as clockwork, she sent him his billet-doux each day. But how did the postman know? Maybe Simon had told him – more than what he'd have told me – or maybe he'd got a whiff of perfume off the envelope. You'd be suspicious of that same blasted postman: he seemed to know more than his prayers. As if we needed another busybody around the area.

I often wonder about Simon, and whether or not he got married to the same *bourd* who'd written to him the time he'd been back here. We haven't seen him since – at least, I haven't. The fellow could well have sneaked in any day I was at work, just to see herself, and I would never find out. In one of his other letters, years back, he sent a photo of himself playing the accordion at a party. He was always good at the music, I'll have to give him that, and it wasn't from me he learned it either. Very few people, I'd go so far as to say, could touch the likes of what he had. Indeed, there was only one other person that I knew who had that same sort of gift.

I looked at the photo for a resemblance to me. But no, he still had his mother's looks. Then I thought that maybe, just maybe, there was something about the way he hunched his shoulders. I tried to remember his walk, the way he'd move his hands while saying something – he did have that gesture, didn't he? – or even the way he might laugh. But how quickly you'd forget people's expressions, even their faces – while others might never leave the spaces of your head, or the dark corners of the room. Wish I could get to sleep now.

THREE

Simon

Hardly seems like I've lived anywhere 'cept here off the Edgware Road. So used to it, the traffic and all. What I'm saying is: this has become my home. On the job six days a week, with a regular wage; along to the club with the wife, Nora, of a Saturday night to meet my mates; and the odd party then: maybe get to play the old squeeze-box. Getting ready to go out, putting on the fresh gear and all, is in itself enough to cheer a body up – there's always something to look forward to. A couple of drinks again on Sunday down the local, then back for an early night to be up for work next morning. Everything regular as clockwork, how I like it; live the good life, it's the only way. Yeah, could've been born here, and every day I pass that school I might've even attended as a nipper.

Doing National Service was what shaped me:

years well spent, a valuable lesson in reality. Too many blokes who came across on the boat spent their time looking over their shoulders, dodging the draft – no insurance number then, no nothing but being beholden to gangsters who operated out of the backs of vans.

Then you got the shops and markets, right under your nose, that stock everything. Modern conveniences at the touch of a button, a wife and kids: what more could a geezer ask for? Unless he's greedy, that is. And like a greed, I had this desire once – a burning desire to get away from home, and from the way of living they had back there. Tell stories all night long, they would, sleep half the next day and hardly a shilling to be had among the lot of them.

This pad may not be the blooming Ritz, but it's central. A long narrow passage from the front door leads back here to the living room, the poky kitchen lean-to we have can be cold – and sometimes smells of gas – and there's only the one bedroom. We've got this yard, see, out the back, where the jacks is – the only one – you wouldn't swing a cat there. The landlady's a crab and she lives upstairs. A demon she was, when we moved here first, but we got to know her and she doesn't bother us now, so long as the rent's paid.

A tight old Jezebel she is too, with the shillings. I've seen her in that moth-eaten fur coat of hers sitting in the front room, in the middle of winter, and not so much as a spark in the grate. She ain't short a few bob, I'll bet, but she don't charge much; that's why we've stayed so long, and it's central — did I say that? It works both ways: she feels safe with us here underneath. We've got our name down with the council for a house, but it may be a long wait. You know how it is: being Irish and all. Don't have the space, though, I had when I was little; I miss that. But what good's all the room in the world, when you ain't got facilities and you're out at back of beyond? They've not even got the roads tarred, least not the ones through Springmount — or so my mum said in her letter. Imagine a car travelling up the laneful of rocks to where I lived. And I'm a damned sight better off here than working for some poxy farmer over there for ten bob a week. Who wants that for hardship? Go back now — get out of it.

Goes without saying though, it would be nice to skip across for a bird's-eye view of the place, and drop in to say hello to my mum. Mind, I've got a soft spot for her. She has a good nature. I'd like to see her before she pops her clogs or grows too batty to recognize me. But as for the old geezer: well, it's like he never was.

And in a way, he never was — I mean: never existed. Hardly ever saw him when I was little, 'cept when he came home at night to sit at the table waiting for her to put a meal before him, and he might or might not grunt. Then off again with himself in ten minutes; always gone he was. Could never figure out where he used to get to, till one time I followed him. I'll say he was a right funny blighter. Not that he ever done me no harm, mind. It's just he had these ways, see: distant, sore almost, like a blooming professor; 'cept he were no way educated. It was his height, and how he always looked away like I wasn't there. Funny, ain't it? And now he don't exist as far as I'm concerned.

Can't understand people like that, not making the best of what they got. Those two could have a royal time there together in the little cottage, snug as bugs in rugs. When he'd come home at night, they could pull up the chairs round the hearth and have a right old natter. You know, good mates, that sort of thing, and get over their differences, like we all have to. Take me and the missus here: we've had our ups and downs, and the odd squabble – no harm in a bit of a spat: clears the air, you know. That mad passion thing never lasts anyway. You got to make the most of life and put the past behind. The problem with them is they never learned to forget, always looking back. Come to think of it, it was that non-stop living the past that I had to get away from.

Got this letter from my mum the other day, saying how she was: feet swollen, arthritis, varicose veins inflamed, and the GP gave her a dressing down over using too much salt. Way overweight, if the last photograph is anything to go by; no wonder she's got trouble on the pins. A pity though. I got some early snaps, the sepia type in the fancy braid surrounds you don't get no more, and she was quite a looker: dark sultry eyes, jet-black hair – I remember that – dainty ankles and the pins were good.

The letter was like one long moan: the cold and damp, the aches and pains, the neighbours' comings and goings, but not a word about the old geezer – or *him*, as she called him when she had to. Though he didn't get a mention, it was *him* she was really grousing about. Her roundabout way of talking hasn't changed.

Even when I was little, my mum was always nattering on about something – not that I blame her, mind. And it was me who had to listen; she never said things to *him*, the one she ought to've been saying them to. I was the target she flung her arrows at, so to speak.

I carried you for just short of the nine months, but you were still an eight-pound pudding at the end, weren't you? She used to say that a lot when he was within earshot; with the emphasis on the *short of nine months* bit, like she was dunning it into his head. With the swellings and stretch marks, I don't know where I am. Can't manage to get my figure back and it's all your fault, you little dickens, you know that. And she'd playfully wag her finger at me. She'd go on like this only when he was around;

talking to *him* through me, she was. And it was always a one-way conversation.

A peculiar bloke, he was, and a bit of a loner; didn't go to the pub to meet his mates – not that I can recall him ever having any mates. He used to walk to that place up the other hill from us, a farmhouse where this dame of about his own age lived on her own. You'd be inclined to think: yeah, the randy old git, he was going there for his bit of . . . you know – how's your father. 'Cept he didn't appear to go inside the house, any time I followed him. Hard to make out his movements in the fading light, and once he went onto her property, he moved like the blooming phantom. Sometimes you'd see his shape passing a window or resting there a while looking in. Your proper peeping Tom was that bloke.

I think he used to go through the farmyard and out to the haggard beyond. Whatever was the attraction out there? Maybe her ladyship wanted to meet him in the hayshed rather than have him in the house, for some reason. You never know now, do you? She might've liked to keep things clandestine, add spice to their trysts. Not speaking from experience, mind, but you'd hear of such things, read about them in magazines. What other reason could he have had for calling there? Goes without saying: I never let on to my mum I'd seen him or followed him. At the time, I didn't suspect him of anything like that. I didn't know then about such things. It was just one of his strange ways, an obsession of his. And boy, did Mr Will Byrne have some of those. A strange bloke, indeed.

And a strange place back there. Might be behind the times as regards facilities and work, but, come to think of it, it's an interesting old world they live in.

FOUR

She was Philly's sister going to school, no more than that. Long hair on the brown side of red, her face covered in summer freckles – that's as much as I can recall of Kate in those early days. Philly and I always waited for one another below at the cross-roads, and the three of us would walk to school together. Before we'd have reached the village, our group would've swollen to about ten. The bigger ones were the group minders – had to be the way, in those troubled times.

It was non-stop listening out for lorries, especially going home in the evenings. With any engine-whine in the distance, we'd make for the nearest field gap, through the gate and get down in the ditch till the motor had come and gone. Not that we couldn't tell the sound of a lorry carrying Tans from that of a Ford or Morris car, but we had to be careful: might be a matter of life and death.

The Tans, here in '20 and '21, were some shower. Every day there was news of looting, burning and murdering in towns and villages round the country. Word had it they'd fired on children from the parish next to us one evening, and those children who were going home from school, across the fields, were lucky they weren't all shot. It was up to Philly and me to look after the others in our group.

It was also the time when we got interested in girls. Or rather, we got interested in the one girl: Maysie Dunne. Ah, hazy Maysie! In the same class in school as Philly and me, she had long jet-black hair, brown eyes and a brown complexion: luscious as a September plum. The loveliest creature in the whole wide world. What a woman she'd turn into. The two of us were under her spell, hovered around her at lunchtimes like flies over a fresh cowpat and played up to her, vying for the least scrap of favouritism.

We pulled and jostled each other to be first into the seat alongside her for catechism class: the opportunity, a right almost, to feel her knee, slip an arm round her waist and sometimes peck her on the cheek, that dimpled cherubic cheek. And off she'd go into the fits of giggles: couldn't be stopped. Not that the old master minded much; he was as deaf as a door, only waiting to retire. I hated it when Philly got to sit with her. You'd feel the lump in your throat; couldn't speak from the *tocht*. Such a sudden rush of dislike for him, you'd have, and you would not be his friend for the rest of that class – no, for the rest of that day – though you'd try not to show it. But the hard truth dawned: he was winning the chase for her affections.

Maysie lived about a hundred yards on the far side of the village. Sometimes, Philly would stay back after school to be with her, do things with her. Worse still: do things to her; fulfil those secret, awful longings he'd've dreamed about from his bed, and satisfy all curiosities about her personal, private make-up. Whereas I was left to mind the others going home; on my own, 'cept for his young sister, Kate. Younger by only a year – but a year at that age is like a generation – Kate was tall; with almost as much authority about her as Philly had. And even then, I had a sense that she wanted to show me how good a job she could do in place of her brother; she wanted me to notice her. But it cut no ice. Maysie, and her round appealing legs and chubby chest, was who I wanted to be with; to make her giggle from the things I imagined I could do to her – much more so than what Philly was probably doing with her right then, when he should have been there with the rest of us. Something gnawed down the pits of my stomach.

He'd won this game all right, with his smiles, the

cajolery, the curly hair and words, especially words, which I'd never have dared utter to Maysie. They were the wrong words, wrong for her; as light as thistledown, they held nothing more than their own sound. He'd sold her a dream – a pup if you like – and she'd fallen for it hook line and sinker. You'd sense as much, even at that age. You'd hope that one day she might realize the folly of his words, and how dwelling on them wasn't good for her. That he wasn't good for her.

But because you weren't as crass – or had a more reserved nature – and lacked the cute curly locks, you were to miss out on being the object of the girl's desires. It stung to see that she looked elsewhere, even if that elsewhere was to my friend – especially if it was my friend. Such gnawing inside would drive a body to act: compel him to find out what was happening. I had no choice but to search them out.

On the way home from school one evening, I gave Kate the excuse of having forgotten something from the shop, and left her to bring home the others. When I got to the school playground, Philly and Maysie weren't there. I stood for a while in the middle of the yard I had never before seen empty of children. The bleakness of the place! I was startled by the thought that there might be something – let me see how to put this – unreasonable about what I was doing there. A fixation of a thing that made my head too heavy to hold up, and like a sharp-edged black streak, it appeared stark against the emptiness all round.

Where were they? I checked that the school door was locked, and went back onto the road to look up and down: listened, but not a soul was stirring. Only Murphy's old sheepdog, which always crooned to the Angelus bell (strange, how every dog Murphy ever had would do the same), came along making thin, sniffing sounds and scratched the ground by the gate with its seared-out paws. When I shushed him away, he scarcely lifted his head but carried on scratching till, in a final show of scorn, he cocked his leg to do his business; then hobbled off like an old man of the world. So, not expecting much, I climbed the fence to the field behind the school.

There they were, the two of them: standing about three steps apart. And, like a pair of small children, they were throwing a sponge ball to each other. Back and forth, back and forth! Philly was so gentle, almost timid, towards Maysie, taking care to lob the ball within reach of her outstretched hands. The funny thing was – no, not at all funny – they had nothing on, not a stitch of clothing. Starkers! Naked in front of each other without the least shame. As if they'd been like that all their lives, had grown up that way; like animals grazing they were as unconcerned as you like. In a field of sunshine of a September evening, the warm light came at them from askew and stroked their young white flesh. I couldn't look at them; had to turn away.

The picture wasn't at all how I had imagined. Didn't know what I had imagined, really, but this wasn't it. It was worse. Imagine, just doing nothing to one another: not what you'd expect of them. Yet how they were with each other was almost unbearable to think about. Like arrows against my insides. I'd wanted to catch them up to something, anything, and all the better if it were a juicy, wicked thing I'd never even heard tell of. But this business of being alone, naked and at nothing, 'cept throwing a ball to each other, was beyond me. With the pure whiteness of flesh and the innocence of their play, they were like lambs in springtime, frolicking through early grass. Could anyone understand the carry-on? Strange, too, the let-down you'd feel, at not having your expectations met.

A picture of the two lambs under a warm sun remained in my head. But after that first shock had eased, picturing them was a bit like looking at some country on the school globe: a far-off country to the warm south, untouched by the hand of winter, where you could never hope to go, not to mind live there, and which you could experience only by imagining it.

The next day in school, it was the usual caper: boys teasing the girls and boys ribbing one another about girls. Philly and Maysie glanced and smiled at each other no more than usual; but when they did, it was in that knowing and secret way which no pair of eyes was alert to – 'cept the one. Nobody else was aware of their antics, or of anything other than the usual good rapport between them. But everyone was aware, without saying as much – too afraid to, at least to my face – that I'd lost the race for Maysie's affections. A sore cut.

But I had my secret knowledge for comfort; to be put to use when-and-if I should think fit. I wouldn't tell on them though; wouldn't stoop to that. Instead, let the hare sit, and wait my chance to avenge the *náire* that should never have been laid at my door.

That day, I let Philly win the race to sit beside Maysie during catechism. What would've been the point in doing anything else? The vying, though, wasn't immediately dropped: appearances had to be kept up – no use in making a complete *googie* of yourself – but I let the edge to our little rivalry taper off till it no longer existed; as if I couldn't be bothered. Or at least, that's the way it would seem to everybody. Besides, I no longer had the stomach for Philly's straightforward sort of competition. The only comfort was in thinking: there's more ways than one to pluck a goose. Aye, pluck the goose like an old town scalder would, after a St. Thomas' Fair. Pluck, pluck, pluck.

I still dreamed of Maysie and her plump, round, luscious body, and what I'd do to her if I got the chance, though Philly had well put paid to such a thing happening. He'd made the highest bid, so she was his. Besides, there was more than a little fondness between them, I will have to admit. This odd attachment continued from those early days, and would surely have lasted – who can tell for how long? – had circumstances not intervened.

In the meantime my desires for Maysie were gradually replaced by a new liking for Kate.

FIVE

In the years after school, Kate went to serve her time dressmaking to old Hetty Murphy in the village. The same Murphys as had the shop, bar and hardware; sold coal, boots and shoes; bought wool in season, and owned the land stretching right up to the mountain commons (their son owns it nowadays). Even the old sheepdog that barked the Angelus was theirs. Whenever the shop got busy, Kate was sent in to help out. She became so good behind the counter, she was made a clerk there full-time. Efficient and courteous though she was, in a quiet way, that's not what first caught my eye. It was the new shape to her body.

She was behind the counter at the far end, in the middle of serving someone, when I went in for an ounce of Clarke's Perfect Plug. Had never paid her notice before. Then all of a sudden, I was looking at her like she was no longer just Philly's sister. Here was a girl in her own right, the new Kate Kelly. Nearly went cross-eyed taking her in, when she stretched up to get a packet of Sweet Afton off a shelf. Flow gently sweet Afton, as the song says.

Two long lines of brown costume flowed evenly from her neck: one front, one rear. The rear line swept down and over the shape of a slight backside, then farther on to show the curves of the backs of her legs – it wasn't easy to look away from those legs. And the line to the front: a slight heaving of the wave-curve to her chest, then straight down like a plumb-bob. Tall, still thin – but not bony: filling out – and that particular walk gave her a finish of elegant harmony. Not so much that she was growing, more like she was being sculpted, into a woman; being hewn into shape before your very eyes. And she certainly caught the eye.

Her manner, too, was different to other girls': quieter, more grown-up, not as giddy and a bit sedate, maybe – hard to define, exactly. On the other hand, when she smiled, she lit up, and when she laughed, it was infectious – your attentions would become firmly hooked. Her manner and looks together made her attractive in a removed sort of way. That she wasn't too approachable only added to her charm: those outfield defences, instead of being a repellent, actually made her more appealing – exclusive and appealing at the same time. She tended to look you straight in the face, weighed up what you were saying, and then accordingly and in her own good time would either smile, or not smile, in response. You got the sense too, talking to her, that it was important to have her on your side; so you had to be in earnest, and take her seriously.

That Sunday after I'd turned seventeen, I decided to walk the banks of the Urrin to check on the growth of some ash trees – Philly had asked me to make a few hurleys for him. Kate was in the distance, on the path by the river I'd intended to take, playing fetch-the-stick with her sheepdog. Felt the old ticker miss a beat, and I stopped in my tracks to inhale the sight of her. In a smart grey-green tweed coat, untied and hanging loose, over a mauve summery dress, she was a delight to watch.

She gave off a certain freshness that was in keeping with the newness of greenery that you'd find everywhere during the month of May. So intense was the foliage that day, you could almost float on its density. And no other sun, either, to match a May sun: warm and full of the promise of high season, and still innocent – not yet tainted by notions of leading the late summer foliage down a road to damnation.

No matter in what direction she threw the stick, the black and white dog would race off, pick it up and every time return it to her. But it didn't just do so from the usual sense of loyalty that dogs are wont to have; you could see that the animal was only delighted to be playing with Kate, and wanted, all ends up, to please her. It was the first time I had identified with a dog. And I got the impression that the animal, though absorbed with chasing through the long grass, was in some strange way making contact with me to pass on its special admiration for the girl. I kept watching Kate while walking towards them. She didn't spot me until I was almost upon them, and when she did her face flushed slightly. And boy, didn't that feel good.

The riverbank beside us was clear of growth. Without hesitation, Kate threw the stick into the river, knowing full well the dog would race in after it. Why did she do that only when I appeared? From the animal's dry coat, it was obvious it hadn't yet been in the water. I'd find out, though, in a minute. There was a touch of wryness to her smile as she looked at me, while Shep splashed through the water. Unchangeable as the passing of time, he came running back with the stick in his mouth to sit meekly on his haunches till Kate would remove it, as much as to say: thank you, and thank you again, for the privilege of having to go in there on my lady's impulse. For what's an old dog's life but to serve young maidens' whims? I was about to tease her over it when Shep took a fit of shaking himself and spewing water – half the bloody river – all over me. The horrid brute! Kate, knowing what would happen, had stepped behind me for cover, and laughed loudly – that infectious laugh that belied her other self in the severe repp uniform. And the devilment of her too!

Well, if she wanted to be playful – in one quick turn and jerk, I caught her and grabbed her up, before she knew what was happening; carried her over to the edge of the water and pretended to throw her in. She was half laughing, half hanging out of my neck and giving out stink, the way that dog of hers would yelp at strangers nearing their house. Will, put me down, she shouted. Put me down, will you? Shep hopped and barked in rings around us, probably in protest at seeing his comely maiden being manhandled.

So you want me to put you down, is it? says I, lowering her closer to the river. What a thrill to feel her arms automatically tighten around the back of my neck in an effort to keep herself out of the water. The tweed collar brushed my chin, and I had a sense of power over what I was doing to her, especially when she protested and called me by my name. Her backside almost touched the river before she stopped protesting. Shoo, she inhaled then, and held her breath. The look on her face meant she realized that maybe I was crazy enough to drop her in – exactly the effect you'd wish for. I simply had to laugh at the moment of fright in her eyes (such a memory is now like a sweet savoury sauce) before I lifted her right up and plonked her back on her feet. You'd wonder should you have dunked her ever so slightly in the water; simply to satisfy the gnawing urge in the back of your head to cross boundaries. Anyway, Kate was smiling again; this time, though, not with devilment – with relief, maybe – and pretended to take a swipe at me.

What are you doing down this neck of the woods? says she.

Oh, we're very nosy today, aren't we?

I'm surprised you're not off chasing girls.

What girls? There are no girls around these parts for a fellow to chase.

Kate gritted her pearly-white teeth, grabbed my shoulders with her fists and made a wide-sweeping *sprock* at me with her leg; as though I'd touched a sore point with her.

I'm surprised, says she, you're not off chasing that Maysie Dunne one; you and all the other fellows. She has yous all sniffing after her, like tomcats. Surely Kate knew that only the one tom got to sniff that particular she-cat. She made another kick at me while holding on to my shoulders.

Sure she's Philly's girl, and what would I want with chasing Philly's girl? As I said it, I tried to hide the smart of an old wound inside.

Kate only laughed. How much did she know then of what for me was a bad memory – the *googie* I'd made of myself over Maysie, that time in school? A lot, it seemed, the way she laughed. How come girls have this way of knowing things about fellows? And here she was using it in mockery, to take me down a peg after I'd dinted her stiff dignity by lowering her to the water. Well, Kate succeeded: all of a sudden, I felt a lot less cocky, and wished I could've cut myself off from her appeal, her looks. A sore woman enough then, this one, should anyone dare step on her toes. I'd have to be careful about where to tread. But then again, maybe she hadn't an inkling of what'd happened to me with Maysie; maybe I was crediting her with too much wisdom, and it was just coincidence that she had laughed then. So some of my cockiness came back.

Listen, I'm going to check on a few ash trees by the river, I said. Do you want to come along? Too much of a challenge and not enough of an invitation was the way it sounded, I knew as soon as the words were out of my mouth. So I added a little dressing to cajole her: Could do with a second opinion, you know.

Was I chancing my arm too soon? Would it not have been better to wait, and spend extra time teasing her; get her to relax more before trying her out? Just wished I'd had some experience of this lark, how long to be playful for, the moment for seriousness and, most importantly, when to make a move. Yeah, the move: timing was everything; get it right, it seemed, and you were away in a hack; get it wrong, well . . . We'd soon find out, though, if I'd got it right. I started to walk on about my business.

A delightful surprise, yet hardly a shock, when Kate came along with me. Without as much as a word in reply to my invitation, she was game to go wherever it was I was headed. It felt scary – well, only a little. Since it was my first time in this situation, alone with a girl, the inclination was to turn on my heels and leg-bail it out of there fast. For this was not going to be just a walk down by the river; more like a dive into its deepest and most dangerous turnhole, where both the lightest and the weightiest things eddy towards the centre, before being pulled underwater for good. It was definitely the start of a journey to a place I'd not been before.

On the other hand, there was the excitement of having Kate's tall elegant shape walk beside you. A thrill to think she'd like you enough to go along, and she had agreed, it seemed, without giving a second thought as to where this walk might lead. For surely she, too, must have known there was more to it than just a saunter along the riverbank. I tried to put a name on it – as impossible as it was to find words that were even close. Was this a proper 'walking out' with a girl? No, not quite that either, nothing arranged; though what other way could you put it? My o' my, a fellow was having his first 'walking out', and an accidental one at that. Yeah, that was the only name for it.

I glanced at her from time to time, maybe more often, and she was smiling and looking back at me. The whole blessed place seemed as if it were changing its colour scheme to a warmer shade of whatever it had been before. All the blooming trees, bushes, things that grew in the grass and the grass itself took on a strange new life. Even the old river was singing to me. Its roaring over mini-rapids and splashing around big mossy stones wasn't noise at all, but music. Gurgle, gurgle, swish. Yes, pure music was what it had been making all along, but had waited till then to suddenly disclose itself and become such an imposing thing. No, imposing isn't quite how it was either; it was more subtle than that: a light-headed intoxication that rose invisibly and spread out like a river fog.

Listen, Kate – by then, even the sound of her name was made up of the most resonant note, and I had to repeat it – Kate, what's the name of that tune? There was a quizzical look on her face, and I was afraid she might allow that I was away with the fairies, hearing things that weren't there. So I tried to whistle a tune she was bound to know the name of, which might seem, in some sort of way, to echo the sound from the river. She'd surely know that old ballad 'The Streams of Bunclody'.

Come here and listen, I said. And, as natural as I

could make it look, I put my arm round Kate's waist to steer her closer to the river. It was in no way natural, though, to do a thing like that; a pure dare to put my arm even near the girl, near any girl. Only a moment did it take for the sensation of my hand on her body to sink in. A bit like flashes inside your head, and the way the tips of your fingers would go all tingly. Maybe I had overstepped the mark again, but to do so had worked previously. And this time, even if nothing else were to come of it, it had been worth the risk to touch and get that shock-feel of her.

But back to the tune. I whistled it softly and low, a sough, to make it gurgle as much like the flowing water as possible, so she might actually pick up on the air. Phooe ei phey thee hay hay phoou, *where the birds do increase* . . .

You sound the same as that loony bird, says she. She was looking at a fat thrush which was perched on a green trunk spanning from one bank to the other, a little downriver from us. And she was right, I did sound more like the plump-breasted bird with its zany chirpy-cheep echoing along the river and through the trees. You'd feel becalmed, though, by the peculiar hypnotic effect of the river. One minute the surface was a million million shards of broken light – enough to blind you – then, after a sudden breeze, the surface darkened down a tone to a more soothing shimmer.

You're daft, you know that? says she, grinning at me. There was that twinge again, but I didn't let on to be affected by her. We both laughed at the idea of the river playing a tune. At least she'd got the drift of what I had been on about. Or maybe it wasn't at that, either, she was laughing. But no matter. That she was enjoying herself was good enough for the moment. The main thing was Kate didn't object to my hand round her waist. No, not a bother on her. Hard to know what to do next. So we stood there, stiffly, for surely five minutes, stealing glances at each other and listening to water music and loony birds. You'd think we were stuck to the spot, scarcely breathing. And, as if by accident almost, our two bodies moved closer together and became more relaxed, a sort of melting. We could've stayed like that for ever. Be that as it may, though, there was a peculiar niggle in the back of my head; like a grey crow watching in the long grass, waiting to pounce and peck the eyes from the young during lambing season.

Show me those ash trees you were talking about, says she, breaking off from the fixed stupor we were in. Kate at once took my hand from her waist and pulled me after her along the path. Until I got used to holding her hand, there was a slightly odd feeling of being a child again; such a harmless act in itself, and you'd like to close your eyes in comfort. Her hand was warm, soothing, and I didn't want to let it go. Then bit by bit, different, more urgent sensations came into play. The path narrowed till we had to walk behind each other, step over thistles and push the briars aside. When we came upon the first ash, growing right in the middle of a clump of thorns, I said nothing; kept going.

Kate stopped in her tracks when a blackbird twittered in the undergrowth. It fluttered madly through the crisp dead wood of previous seasons' growth and rose to the safety of a branch. As if in sympathy, a waterhen went skittering off down the river. Kate's hands flicked to her head, like a child in delight at seeing a new plaything, and you just knew, through this surprise alone, she'd become aware of the grandeur of the place. Almost at that moment, back along the path, a flurry of the previous year's leaves lifted, fluttered about and then immediately died down: a *shee gwee*, if ever I saw one. A thing that sticks in your brain, and only afterwards, when it's too late, you realize its magic: the moment that was. One of those delayed-reaction moments; if you could only return to savour it, and especially to see the thrill of it register in the girl's face. But such excitement, you were sure, would again appear on Kate's face (at seventeen, you're not yet aware that magic seldom recurs, and definitely not within such a short space of time). When we reached the clearing, with luck the rabbits would be out sitting in the long grass. On sensing us they'd scurry off, and the sight of so many white tails bobbing, scuttling in all directions, would surely set her heart racing again.

The next thing on the agenda. Stand back there and make room for the tree inspector! Let's take a close look now; eye up the stem for straightness, feel the lower trunk where it goes to ground and see if the grain is suitably curved for hurley bosses. But there was no need for the big examination; I'd known all along the trunk was ideal for hurleys. Three planks it would surely yield, maybe four – in the raw – allowing for waste cuts on either side. But I had wanted Kate to notice. That's why I went round saying: What do you think now? Look, feel the bark, it's as smooth as your face. When I put my hand on her cheek, Kate went a little shy. I caught her hand and placed it on the tree bark, then back to her cheek. Well, isn't that right now? I said playfully. I kept my hand on her face. Amazing how soft it was. Well come on, tell me how many hurls can be got from the tree? She didn't answer; she bit her lower lip, letting on to be figuring it out. When she tilted her head down slightly and flicked them big eyelids at me, I couldn't resist my urges.

Feck this business of overstepping boundaries, I said to myself: the moment is now or never. So I caught Kate's hands and pulled her close, looked into her surprised eyes and touched her with my mouth. Put the gob on her, I did. Despite my clumsiness, she didn't object – you might say she responded willingly – and I wondered why the hell I'd been the least bit anxious before. That, in the beginning, the two of us were unhandy at groping only served to cover up the embarrassment we might've felt. We soon moved – stumbled over each other, rather – from the standing position to lying on the grass, and became more settled, less hurried. The only thing by way of discomfort was the bias binding on the hem of her tweed coat, as it lay into my cotton shirt. It was an end to ash trees and hurleys for that day, when the gatchying got going in earnest.

Later on, walking home, we held hands right up to where the gate led onto the road from the well field. I climbed over first – too much bother to open it – glanced up and down the road to see that there was no one coming and lifted Kate down with my arms round her waist. She got a good tickling, too, before she was let go, and giggled loudly. The hair on her head, all tasselled, hid a laughing mouth and the soft wild glint to her eye.

Oh ho, what have yous been up to? this mocking voice shouted from out of the ditch on the other side of the road. About as welcome an intrusion as thunder on Midsummer's Day.

I had thought there was nobody around; hadn't spotted the big hoor lying there in the gripe. He leaped up like a cow in heat, as if he was going to attack us. The round belly bulged out over the trousers belt – strange: he didn't wear gallowses – as, legs apart, he hopped sideways on the stony road in front of us. He had a walking stick raised over his head ready to strike and I was so sure he was going to attack, I whipped off my coat and furled it round my arm to ward off the blows – the first thing to do when confronted by a thug wielding a knife: so my brother, Mylie, had said. I pushed myself in front of Kate and faced up to the hoor. But he didn't attack. He only waved his stick in the air to mimic Father Cormick, who used to walk the roads in search of courting couples and chase them from their lairs in ditches after Sunday night concerts in the school. 'Cept Father Cormick used a nobbly blackthorn; this fellow carried a great fancy stick.

Get away from here, you hoor, I roared at the stranger. Mind your own business before you get that stick larruped round your neck.

Whoa now, slow down, says he. You've a bad tongue in your head for a young fellow. A bad word betrays a nasty mind.

He looked at Kate and feigned a sad face. Ah, my child! says he. In what carnal acts and indecent activities of beastly behaviour have you been indulging in yonder thicket? Do you not realize, my forlorn one, that such unbecoming conduct can only lead to the ruin of your blessed sanctity, and the loss of your immortal soul? Have you no idea of the woes and torments of fornicators, indeed of all debauched lechers, who've trod these same insidious paths of pestilence before you? Let me tell you, they are burning in the black pits with the damned, roasting for all eternity. Oh, you're damned, I say, damned. I get the smell of roasting flesh this very minute. Show me your hand, my child, let me sniff to see how far down that well-trodden path you've gone. Ah, my perverted one, do you know that cooked human tastes quite like roast pig, of a Friday? And right now, somewhere on the rare side of done, you smell like a tasty morsel of pork steak. So repent, my little piggy child. I say repent, before it's too late.

Whoever the fellow was, he had old Father Cormick's manner off to a tee. He then stretched out his arms, the stick in one hand, just as his reverence would do on coming across an unfortunate couple in a ditch. The tail of your man's shirt flew out, and Kate laughed.

And woe betide the sinful mocker, says he, chanting again and pointing his stick at her like it was a sword he was about to stab her with. Then he stepped back, turned and fecked off down the road with himself. Some man to walk: he took long strides, with the beetle-crushers thumping off the ground like he was in the army. As he lolloped away, his belly and shoulders flopped to the rhythm of forward movement. If you didn't know any better, you'd say he was a hard ticket to be frightened of.

He kept up the sermonizing, and the farther away he went, the louder he chanted, while waving his stick. A final roar out of him, before disappearing round the bend onto the bridge below: Take warning, my sinful child, be careful.

Who the hell is that lug? I turned to ask Kate. But she was in a knot laughing, pointing at me with the coat still wrapped around my arm. So instead of being her gallant protector, I was back to being that *googie* in her eyes. Was that all the thanks you'd get for your efforts at chivalry? I felt a touch of anger.

Do you not know who that is? says she, at last composing herself. Imagine you don't know Cha. Where have you been? Sure everybody knows Cha.

The scorn in her manner again, with emphasis on the *you*, this time bespoke a certain haughtiness, which I'd noticed about her ways in the shop. It somehow took from the tone of the afternoon we'd had.

That was the first time for me to come across Cha Cha Tobin. He was just home from America, the only emigrant I knew to've made the return trip. It turned out he was mad into the music.

Sure, he's harmless, says she. But he didn't seem that to me. And as for Kate herself: she was in no way harmless either.

SIX

The next Tuesday evening, there was music going on inside Kellys' house; it could be heard from the road. I turned in the gateway, across the yard and into the porch. Philly barely glanced from the instrument he was so taken up with. Head tilted on a skew, his right ear was as near as he could get it to the sound's source. And a second accordion was being played. It was in the hands of none other than that lug from the Sunday, Cha Cha Tobin.

He was giving Philly the first – or was it the second? – part of some new tune. They went through it together once. With a couple of adjustments, Philly slowly repeated the tune, and then played it through at the correct tempo. The other fellow joined in, and the two accordions played in unison; till soon it was hard to tell who had learned from whom.

From the time Philly got his hands on the tune, it was the same as watching the world being created, or what Creation must've been like. All you could do was stand and stare. That's how it seemed anyway, standing inside the kitchen door, before I got a chance to take in the rest of the place – as you'd normally do when entering anyone's house. From his fingering of single notes to the tune's phrasing and on to when he played it through without a slip, the progress was awesome, and that was only the start. Then came the music proper, the magic – the end of the Seventh Day when all things had been put in place, and the world at last came fully into being. Definitely, that tune was brought into its own when Philly got his hands on it. Your head would get taken over by the strain that came at you in waves; it would stupefy the dumbest of creatures. Such damned talent!

Cha Cha winked and nodded in approval, and Philly smiled back. Cha's mouth opened to say something, but Philly gave a draw on the instrument's bellows, fanning it out like a hand of cards. The noise was wicked enough to prevent your man from talking, and when he opened his mouth a second time, Philly did the same thing. Cha Cha snorted out laughing, his belly shook and he slapped his hand off his knee. They both laughed. In that instant, the colloguing that had gone on between them through their playing was exposed, confirmed. And I'd just stepped into some sort of *cogar mogar*, a reminder of the time we used to compete for Maysie Dunne's attentions. I was an outsider again.

You'd know, too, when you're under scrutiny. A certain heat touches the inside of your head; you can sense the eyes going through you. I sidled over to sit on the wooden form beside the stairs, and when I looked up, sure enough, there was that lug watching me. His eyes then moved to Philly's accordion, as much as to say: I was only there looking around the room, when an object arose before my eyes, some paltry, human obstacle that I couldn't be bothered looking at. Diddley-idle-didle-idle-dom.

The instruments bellowed on and, for an instant, I had a strange sensation of being outside myself, outside of even the house and looking back at it; listening to lonely accordions cry within, as the whole shebang of Kellys' faded off into the cold night. A shivery sensation of foreboding.

Kellys' was probably the most open of rambling houses. Without bothering to knock, you'd just march in and sit down as you would at home, no questioning looks towards the non-regular, the occasional caller. Nanny and Pat Kelly's was like that.

Nanny's was the stool by the fanners, while Pat

sat across from her, in the dark soot corner, out of everybody's way. And since he was always in black, you'd have to look a second time to check it was Pat there. He wore a black wide-rimmed hat — to ward off the falling soot, it was said. Came to life only when he had somebody to talk to about ploughing, prices at the Borris fair or barley yields. It's been a good year for the barley, Pat Kelly would say. The capers of young people mattered little to him.

Nanny Kelly more than made up for him though. She concerned herself not only with what Philly and Kate did, but also with what everyone was up to. And what are you doing with yourself these times? she'd ask, or ask somebody else about you. Despite her dowdiness, she seemed to think she was still a young one of twenty-five. Whereas old Pat knew his place in time: a relict of another era, who didn't want to be forever sticking his nose into the affairs of the young, whom he probably didn't like much anyway. Most people saw Nanny Kelly as a big-hearted woman, such interest she showed for the welfare of her fellow beings.

I didn't see her the way others did. Of course she was interested in people, especially the young, but a curiosity in her children's friends only meant she was looking after her own brood. An instinctive thing; no more than how a collie bitch with a litter of pups in the barn would behave. And friends or callers to the house were simply companions for her own lot, even yardsticks by which she'd measure how well her children were coming along.

Any time I'd met that woman, when Philly and I were going to school, it was always questions. What sums are you doing now? she'd ask; even though she'd already have known, since Philly and I were in the one class. And are you able to do them? That's really what she wanted to know, to measure Philly's progress. No, Mrs Kelly, I can't manage them old proper fractions at all, at all; they're like double Dutch to me. And to see her face light up then! 'Cept for that time Philly had wiped my eye with Maysie: a flipping genius at the sums, I'd become then the next time I met her. And the look Philly threw me, like thunder. A sweet moment that.

Needless to say, Nanny Kelly wouldn't take kindly to me seeing Kate. Too much to expect. A farmer's daughter associating with a carpenter from the cottage in the lane! Even if Kellys' was little more than a few acres, and mostly brow. She wouldn't dare tell you to your face, but you'd pick it up from the sideswipes she'd make. No different to any woman of her standing, Nanny's notions of grandeur were as fixed and sharp as the corner granite of their cowhouse.

You'll have nothing to do with the likes of him and that's that, she'd tell Kate. Have sense, girl; you can do better for yourself, surely. There's consumption in that house.

*   *   *

On this particular Tuesday evening, I was there, *moryah*, to talk to Philly about the ash trees growing by the river. He'd asked me if I thought they might be ready to be toppled.

Hello stranger, says Nanny, when the music broke. From her throne beside the fanners, she was looking at me for any face-tic at her 'stranger' remark, or any other giveaway to show she'd cracked the outer skin to lay bare the secret scraps she needed to titillate herself with. Made me wary, she did. Since the real reason I'd landed on her kitchen floor was to see Kate and give her the beck to meet outside later. Fat chance, if Nanny Kelly were to be by the fire, guarding her litter like the old collie bitch – at least that animal knew when to stop suckling her pups. So, to keep Nanny from cracking open my shell, I focused my look just to one side of her face, and avoided catching her eye. With a bit of luck she wouldn't spot the ploy.

And how is your poor mother? says she. Haven't seen her in ages. Does she ever stir outside the door? Sure, the *craythur* had it tough: left alone in the world to rear a family. Unfortunate to lose her man so early in life. A good man he was, too – ah, that accursed disease: taken half the country, it has. Where did they ever get yous two brats from? Yourself and that brother of yours, Mylie – will he ever be any good for anything, that fellow? She ought to get out of the house more often: the sunlight would do her the power of good – now, tell her I said that. Very pale she was the last time I met her.

My mother is fine, Mrs Kelly, I said. Hello, Mr Kelly. How are you going on, Philly? But I ignored the lug, Cha Cha Tobin. You know those trees, Philly, you were talking to me about . . .

Before I had a chance to finish, my siren landed in the door. Our eyes met, and her face went to pink and then to red. I got self-conscious too; embarrassment's as contagious as the bloody measles. We swapped knowing looks and bashful smiles, like any young *aroons* might give each other when they mistakenly think no one else is privy to their secret language – you'd think nobody had ever been down this road before. And the fact that the accordions hadn't restarted only highlighted our awkward signals. I felt a tingle of unease across my shoulders. Nanny Kelly, I'd bet, knew sign language.

So that's why you've called to see us? says Nanny.

Well, blast her to hell! The quiet of the place seemed to become more quiet. Kate's mouth opened at the shock that her mother might have read her face, understood our expressions and, worse, guessed there was something between us. She, too, must've been disgusted with herself for not being more careful. But it turned out to be a false alarm.

And what trees might they be now? says Nanny.

Oh Mother! Philly snapped at her. Just a few ash trees down by the river that I asked Will to look at for me.

Thanks, Philly. Could've forgiven him almost anything for opening his mouth at that moment and cutting her short. Kate was so relieved she threw me a quick smile.

The old one was about to focus her attention elsewhere. Well, Kate, how did your work go today? says she, as she jerked her seat away from the direction of her son, vexed with him. And would you like your dinner now? Nanny went on playing to her own spite. There's spuds left in the big pot beside your father, and bacon on the plate under the saucer on the dresser. Sit yourself down and I'll put it out for you. You must be tired after the day, daughter. It was hard to tell if making a fuss over Kate would have even the slightest pay-back effect on her son, certainly not as much as was intended; or if it did, Philly never let on.

Next, there was a caterwaul from an accordion; this time it was Cha's. Do you know, Philly, says he, there's this hymn that's all the rage in America? The lug's voice filled the kitchen.

I'm gonna lay down my sword and shield,
Down by the riverside,
Down by the riverside,
Down by the riverside.

> *I'm gonna lay down my sword and shield,*
> *Down by the riverside.*
> *I ain't gonna study war no more.*
> *I ain't gonna . . .*

The insolent bastard! You'd feel like wrapping the instrument round his fat *scrogall*. Having finished the song, he talked about America, his work in a steel mill the whole size of a small farm and the tunes he'd learned from the sons of famine emigrants. Numbers, says he, not heard in this country for a hundred years, maybe more. And who could argue with him? One night in a bar room in Pittsburgh – such a faraway ring to the name, almost exotic – Cha had bumped into an old Carlow man who, as a boy during the Famine, had crossed to America on a barque out of the port of Ross. The rest of the family had died of fever within a year of their arrival.

Cha talked to Philly as if nobody else in the room mattered. The old man, says he, whipped out a tin whistle from inside his topcoat and played the tune that you've just learned. His old eyes watered up as he told me he'd first heard it from a travelling piper, John Cash, at the fair of Borris in the County Carlow.

Which fair day was that, I wonder? says a voice from the soot corner. The mention of a fair in Borris had awoken Pat Kelly's interest. His sudden remark cut across the *plausey* from Cha.

Philly reached across to the dresser, picked up the green tin of Zam-buk, prised it open and rubbed some of the ointment on the base of his thumb, which the accordion's leather grip had blistered. He put the tin back on the dresser beside the box of Rinso – *Well begun is half-done*, was how the box read.

Cha and Philly took to their instruments, and once more played St Anne's Reel. It had an eerie feel to it: something of a frail old man coming into the room and wailing at the rest of us about the loss of his family. Strange how some reels, fast and lively though they are, have, through the strict regularity of their beat, a peculiar haunting make-up that you won't get in the wailing of even the most plaintive lament – slow and all though the melody may be. Reels for sadness; slow airs are for looking into ladies' eyes.

The lug's head was bent over; his eyes couldn't be seen. Without warning, he stood up, packed away his instrument and took off with himself out the door, without as much as a goodbye or a nod to anyone. Left looking wide-eyed at each other, we were, to wonder what was the matter with him.

Of course, it would take Nanny Kelly to put words to Cha's *taom*. What came over that fellow all of a sudden? says she. Did someone say something to take his biscuit? She crooked her head and glanced sideways at Philly to see his reaction before she'd dart him some more. That fellow's a bit of a queer hawk I'm thinking, says she, hesitantly as if to measure the weight of her remark.

Philly took the bait. Mother, why do you always have to comment on the things you know nothing about? says he.

No reply from her; just an inkling of a smile: she knew she could still rise him. With a man's hobnails on, Nanny Kelly stretched out her black-stockinged leg towards the ashes, and thumped a coarse-barked baulk of old furze farther into the fire. Sparks rose and crackled, miffed-like, in an arc of display, and she pulled her leg back quickly. She then glanced over at me – the outsider in the room. You'd have to watch what you'd say in this house lately, or you'd get the nose bitten off you, says she.

I didn't get to give Kate the beck to meet me outside; so I took my leave of the household and went home.

The next Sunday, I again set out to walk the banks of the Urrin. There was Kate on ahead, picture-perfect, playing fetch-the-stick with her dog: exactly how I had hoped it might be. But while I watched her from the gate, there was a sense of something missing. The picture was too predictable; lacked the thrill of accidental surprise, with a hint of disappointment I couldn't stave off.

Are you going to look at ash trees with me today,

Kate? I said, skitting with her. We might recoup the newness. She swiped at me with her leg again, and we headed off along the path by the river. Predictable, and all so effortless.

When we reached the spot where we'd ended up the previous Sunday, we immediately got down to the business of courting. At first she seemed uneasy with my urgency; so I said: hands slow down. But Kate was soon into the swing of things; her hands became as avaricious as mine and every bit as demanding. I was confused by this: not at all how I had pictured the girl from the shop. Almost as if she were a different girl – two different women present to my fingertips: mighty eh? Her wild insistence was somewhat off-putting.

Sunday after Sunday, me and Kate spent the summer long down by the river, courting. And despite it being a season of freedom and discovery, I felt a growing unrest that betimes almost simmered. A grey crow of a thing watching in the long grass.

No one knew about me and Kate, and nobody was suspicious, 'cept for the lug, Cha Cha. Kate eventually told Philly – she reluctantly admitted it when I quizzed her – but he wasn't the type to make much of it. Sooner or later, though, her mother would find out. Aye! Since I wasn't a farmer's son, I'd never be accepted as good enough for that woman's daughter.

Maybe it was just as well, or I'd have had to walk

out with Kate in the normal way. A couple to be
watched. A right pair of *googeens* stepping along the
road of a Sunday afternoon, with ne'er a chance to
slip behind the ditch for a court.

SEVEN

Simon

Talk about facilities! You can travel anywhere in this town. Five minutes' walk to the Tube, or down to the bus stop, then off with you to where you want to go.

Back home in Ireland, it'll be a thousand years before they'll have the likes of that. When I was there, it was all bikes; mightn't see a motor from one week to the next, though my mum says in her letters, motor cars are getting plentiful: Beetles and Minis and Morris Minors. She's got the names right-on, and whenever somebody buys a car, or changes their old one, it's a spur for her to sit down and write to me. I know more about the mode of transport of the people over there, even though I've been gone fifteen years, than I do of my neighbours hereabouts. But they'd want to do something about them roads – can't imagine the council ever getting round to laying tar on that lane up our house.

The one thing I'm grateful to them back there for is the music, or, to be more precise, the squeeze-box. At this stage, I can walk into any Irish pub in London and the barman will ask: Hey, Simon, did you bring your accordion? Worth two pints a visit in any establishment. To sit in on a session where all the faces are strange, it's like we've been mates all our lives, after a few tunes. Always a new reel or jig to be picked up or swapped. You can tell by his playing if the piper's from Kerry, the flute player's from Sligo or the fiddler's from Donegal.

That fat bloke, Cha Tobin, was the one back home who taught me. A bleeding character, if ever I saw one. He didn't like my old lad, Will Byrne, any more nor I did; an odd thing then that he should've gone out of his way to teach me. There wasn't much teaching, mind: it came naturally. Called to the house one day when I was little, he did, and spoke to my mum. Teach him the accordion, says she right off, I want him to play the accordion. They seemed to know each other from before my time; had a long chat: you know, down memory lane, all that. He'd call about once a week, during the day when my old lad wasn't there. Became a dab hand, I did, with that instrument. And Cha also taught me to play the whistle. Don't forget, says he, the whistle is always your first instrument.

After an hour's lesson, my mum would send me up to the village for something nice. She'd just about have the tea wet when I'd get back. A china cup and saucer from a wedding present, she'd place before him on the yellow oilcloth – the brightest item in the house. As always he'd say to her: I don't want no tea in no cup; reminds me too much of Amerikay. And he'd point to an old crackly mug with a blue rim hanging off the dresser.

I didn't suspect any hanky-panky between them, though I was never to open my mouth about his visits, or the accordion lessons, to the old lad, to no one. She warned me. I wouldn't have done so anyway, out of loyalty. Cha said there was only one other he'd known to've had as good an ear as me. I remember he was looking at my mum as he said it. Had she been a pupil of his then? She was probably a student all right, of something other than music – I'll say no more. Nah, I don't blame her. The geezer she was married to was no ornament.

Mustn't be flippant about them though. Can't really see how they'd've stripped to the skin and hopped into the scratcher the minute I was out the door; their bellies would've been in the way. *I stripped to the skin with the Darky Flynn way down upon the Isle of Grain*. My mum and Cha! Not on your life. It was more a friendship thing – platonic is what it's called nowadays. *No, we're not 'aving it off, we're 'aving a platonic relationship*. Bloody hell! The atmosphere in our house would come to life when he called. He made her laugh like I'd never known her to laugh. When I made a slip with my fingers, he made a joke of it. What a way to learn! He lifted the shadows from over her, least for a while.

As much as I liked my mum, it was no pleasure being round her. She was as glum as a wet winter, and that type of thing is catching: before you realize it, you feel yourself sinking into a bog-hole. So, to have Cha call was like our place having a spring-clean, or a face-lift. Getting back from the shop, it was great to go up the lane, into the yard and, from round the gable, hear the two of them chirruping inside like a pair of skylarks. I'd linger there at the corner for a moment and take in the jollity, same as you'd stop to absorb a winter's sun. Didn't understand much of what was talked about, but no matter, it felt good. Pity the house couldn't've resounded like that always. Gossamer days.

Will you ever forget how sharp he could be with the tongue, says my mum.

Sharp? says Cha. He could cut you to pieces, and you wouldn't even feel it. There was a certain individual, we'll mention no names, and any time they met, our friend used to hop off him; but your man was too dense to notice. Although maybe, you'd know better than most about that same tongue.

Just heard Cha muttering the bit about a tongue as I was going in the door, and I didn't know if she'd heard it. I'm not normally good at remembering what people say, but as the years pass, scraps of chatter come back. And I'd hear voices from that time, the way the notes of a forgotten tune would ring in your ear, suddenly out of no place. An odd thing that. Maybe the picture of the tongue Cha talked about had burned itself into my brain – burning tongues and all that, from the Penny Catechism days. Bits of poems and tables, too, have a habit of flashing back, especially after a few pints.

What Cha had meant though, her knowing better than most about a certain tongue, puzzled me for years, till I lost my innocence probably. And when it came to me – that's the way I grew up: for ages wondering about something, and then the answer would come right out of the blue – I at once thought I knew it all, everything about everybody. So my mum hadn't always been an old drip; she'd garnered a little of the ways of the world about her. A pity, though, I can't remember more of their chats: then we'd have some snippets to chew on, eh?

Anyway, it was never easy to pick up on their conversations. Always the same with adults, isn't it, when kids walk in the room? The discussion gets removed into the lingo of ahems, nods and laughs, the way a knife gets picked off the floor out of the way of a toddler. Those two were brilliant at it;

seldom had I a clue of what they were on about. Not only that, but they could carry on talking in two languages at the same time. Cha, while giving me the fix on some tune, would say: Simon, don't hold that note for quite so long. And in the same breath, without turning to my mum by the fire, he'd say: That individual was spotted in a certain place again the other night. All gobbledegook to me.

Was he! What night was that? she'd ask.

You nearly have it, Simon, that's it; now go on to the next bit. Night before last.

We must be nearing a full moon so, she'd reply. What time was this?

Never let yourself be tempted to rush a hornpipe. Remember the dancers and picture the steps in your head. I don't know; it was late enough. Don't be daft, woman, too much light when there's a full moon; he wouldn't risk that.

And my mum would laugh in that peculiar way of hers that you'd know wasn't a laugh – more a crisp scoff, a measured huh huh huh. What she some-times might quip was: Is that a fact? You don't say. Worst thing in the world is to lose out on a yarn, and miss the laughter; taught me a lesson: always make sure to listen when anyone cracks a joke, to get the punchline.

The great news-chats between Cha and my mum gradually eased off, and had ended by the time I was eleven or twelve. And the lessons stopped round that time. I got too interested in other things – you know yourself, when you're that age – to be bothered with music, and I saw less of Cha. He didn't stop calling to our house, though; it's just that he called earlier. When I'd get home in the evening, I'd know if he'd visited that day. That's the thing about merriment: it leaves an afterglow in a place, in the walls and the furniture cracks, and on my mum's face.

EIGHT

The cottage I live in now is where I was reared and lived with my mam and Mylie, my older brother, all those years ago. Before that, it was my father's house, until his death when I was ten. It's just a couple of hundred yards up the lane off the road to the village. My father had built a lean-to to the upper side of the house, as a car-shed, and another separate outhouse to one side of the small yard, for use as a workshop.

That workshop, more than anywhere else, had something of my father about it. And since the start of my trade, it was where I'd kept my tools. Nice and peaceful in there under the lamplight, being left alone to dream of Kate and the summer we'd spent by the river. I especially liked to go in there, to get away, when Mylie's friends – and did he have some queer coons as friends – would call to the house. One fellow in particular, you'd think, had no home of his own: he was in our house so often.

Through the following winter and spring, Jim Rowe used to call to our house every other night. Himself and Mylie were thick as thieves, ever since the Troubles. They had served in the same brigade company in the War of Independence against the occupying British forces. When the Anglo-Irish Treaty was signed in December 1921 to give Ireland back her freedom, many people could not accept its terms. To get independence for only twenty-six counties out of thirty-two was a disaster. We became a free state rather than a free country, and civil war broke out between the anti-Treaty side and the supporters of the agreement. Since the anti-Treaty crowd were not the ones who'd taken over power from the English, they were by far the weaker group. Himself and Mylie had taken the anti-Treaty side and were on the run from the Free State soldiers. The same unit, which included Jim Rowe's two brothers, had stayed intact through both wars.

Whenever those four were together, they made up an odd, unpredictable bunch; like they were still soldiering, hadn't swallowed the idea of a peacetime nor were ever likely to. All fighting had ceased in May '23, nearly a year previous. Are you sure there's no job lined up? one of the Rowes asked their brother Jim, who had led the company.

All operations have ceased, was the reply.

Nothing coming up?

All operations have ceased. Bury your weapons. Orders from the top.

A change, though, in Jim's tone of voice: the lack of vigour to his usual rasping out of instructions had suggested that he didn't altogether agree with these *orders from the top*.

And all weapons weren't buried in bogholes either. Nothing of the sort. Take Mylie. He'd routinely lift his darling out from where he kept her in the corner of a wardrobe, wrapped in a white Portia flour-bag. *She* was how he referred to the rifle, and he minded it like *she* was a woman. He'd spend ages cleaning, oiling and fondling the bitch. The same with the Webley he kept wrapped in newspaper inside the specially made up oilcloth pouch, and hid over the bedroom ceiling – hidden is right: the first place you'd look, on seeing the gap in the sheeting. A blade in a scabbard, rosary beads and a penal cross of bog oak were all tangled up with a dozen or more odd bullets and stuffed into a Kerry Maid Toffee tin – without the cover – in the top drawer of the dressing-table. Nothing had been got rid of. He'd grab and hold on to the sides of the dressing-table then, when an unexpected fit of coughing came on, and wait a few moments to get his breath back. A cough that he couldn't throw off, from wettings and living rough, was what he'd got for all his Troubles.

No word? The first thing that was said, every time those fellows met. And *no word* was usually the answer: how they greeted each other.

No word?

No word.

A whole minute's quiet then to absorb what it meant this time. Was there a shade of difference in tone from the last time: the least bit of news in the wind or, indeed, anything implied? But *no word*; that was it. When the conversation would pick up, there was never much said, anyway, even with the four of them present. Time together was laced with long silences, and they said only what had to be said. They'd shared some near misses while on the run, and had learned to rely on ways of signalling other than speech. As finely tuned as the hairspring of a watch, they were: a raised eyebrow for curiosity, an up-tempo march whistled to arouse passing interest in something and a rasped-out cough to demand serious attention or as a warning – boy, had they acquired some death-rattle rasping coughs. A slow air showed boredom, nothing happening. So, little need for small talk, and long silences between them were in no way awkward, only to the unwary outsider.

Saturday night in our house was a time for polishing shoes. Jim Rowe would produce this pair of boots from the brown paper under his arm, Mylie would take out his *specials* from the cubby hole under the dresser, and with newspapers on the floor they'd spend the next hour polishing, spitting and shining.

Why do yous always have to spit on them? I asked Jim.

Brings up the shine, says Mylie, answering for him, as if Captain Rowe needed a spokesman and wasn't to be bothered with silly questions from civilians. The look Mylie threw: as much as to say, this is soldiers' business, and though you are my brother, you're still an outsider. The secrecy there was even to polishing boots! Oh, an exclusive club; you'd wonder what a fellow would have to do to get in.

One time, Jim Rowe had pulled out two pairs of wine-coloured gaiters and handed one pair to Mylie.

Are they for me?

Who do you think they're for, your mother?

Wouldn't she look well! Where'd you get them?

Aha! That'll do now – more fecking secrecy.

Jim Rowe's little finger didn't know what his fore-finger was doing half the time. They were all like that, those rebel fellows – wild rapparees, *moryah*, who wouldn't tell you the time of day if you asked them, in case it would betray the cause.

Some yokes, those gaiters! The hour's polishing of a Saturday night became an hour and a half. They'd miss Mass sooner than forego polishing the gear.

Once or twice only, the spats were worn. People laughed, under their breath of course – would you blame them? – but the two copped it. Oh, sensitive out, those boys! Mylie's ended up, thrown, in an old tea chest in the coalshed, dumped with the rest of the worn-out clogs. It was hard to know what notion had got into them: gaiters had never been part of their rig-out during active service.

Because I was a brother of Mylie's and he'd been Jim Rowe's lieutenant, they regarded me as some sort of protégé, future material in the fight against the oppressor – cannon fodder, or at least a mouth to broadcast their notions. I was scarcely out of primary school when it was all dinned into me: the sad history of our land – and sadder yet, having to listen to them telling it. From the Normans to the Flight of the Earls, from the Penal Laws to 1916 in the GPO. And, because it was local, the 1798 rising was a speciality.

Both Mylie and his captain were experts on the Battle of Vinegar Hill – the site was ten miles away. With backs straightened and tears in their eyes, almost, they'd look eastwards to Vinegar Hill the way a compass swings north, and sermonize like Father Cormick on Sunday morning. About how an untrained, ill-equipped and peace-loving bunch of people had been goaded into taking on the might of an empire, and nearly prevailed; how the Yeos had burned and ravaged the countryside afterwards. If only they'd organized properly, says Mylie, and carried on a guerrilla campaign like ours, we'd've been shot of the tyrant long ago.

We're still not shot of them, Jim Rowe said. Ah, the cast-iron venom of the man; he hadn't been their company boss for nothing. His tongue was sharp when needs be.

You're dead right, says Mylie, showing his leader due deference. But if your man Mick Collins hadn't sold us out, we might be rid of them.

Collins, it has to be said, did his bit before the Treaty, says Rowe, his voice sharp as a blade. Between members of the one unit even, there were differences ready to flare up, were it not for the influence of old regimental order. A mix of patriotism and hatred would seethe like a volcano in a rebel champing at the bit for activity. But Rowe knew when to hold his rage and how to take the steam out of a situation.

I suppose, Mylie, you'll be heading for town Friday night to check out them Scalder women. A big night in the Athenaeum, I believe. Listen, young fellow – was the rebel leader suddenly talking to me? – I don't suppose you'd care to come along? I heard you got a new bike. Where did you buy it?

Inside in Kenny's, says I.

It's a Rudge so, says he. Do you know that same building was there in 'ninety-eight? It wasn't bikes

92

they were dealing in then, let me tell you. Kenny's for bikes, Kenny's for pikes.

Oh shit! I hoped it wasn't going to be another sermon.

My mother was none too pleased to hear him ask me along to town. And she let it be known.

For heaven sake, Ma, he's seventeen years of age, says Mylie, when she'd finished going on about the wiles of townies, dangers on street corners and the chances of being beaten up. Any danger in town was nothing compared to the risks of being near the pair of rebels before me. Take a hold of yourself, will you, Ma? He reminded me of how Philly had put old Nanny in her place. This, though, was different. Mylie was only laughing, mocking my mam's silliness. Nor could you compare her to Philly's old one. Mam's face was waxen, her hair the colour of quicklime, and she was out of touch with the world.

Will you be responsible when anything happens to him? says she to Mylie, and replace his bike when it gets stolen? Tell me that, you that knows so much? Despite her frailty, my mam wasn't going to give in easily. For her, it wasn't a debate: these things would happen, all of them together on the one night. The new bike would be stolen, I'd get kicked to death on a street corner and, to top it all, some floozy would spread her legs – oh, the relish of it – to wangle her ways, and the poor old cottage mother would never see her son again. Mark my words, says she. Always weird when she said that, *mark my words*; as though she were inviting disaster, to be proven right.

My mam and her funny old forecasts. She had her own horrors though, left over from the time Mylie'd been on the run. She would've had to live with the idea that each time he'd go out the door, her next sight of him might be on a stretcher, sporting a hole in his forehead. But it was from her, it seemed, that the life force had been drained.

Just as well then she never found out about the things those two feckers had done, as they said, to make a man of her youngest son. Like the frosty night the bowsies came in drunk, bundled me out of bed, lugged me down the lane and across to the bridge; told me to strip and then dumped me over the bridge into the icy water. Laughed down from the bridge, they did, as I sloshed my way to the bank. Another night, I awoke with a gun to my head, and out I had to go in my pelt to run around a field for half an hour, no boots or stockings on and three inches of snow on the ground. She didn't know about the risks I'd taken, either, carrying messages for them while they were on the run.

The two thicks deserved their lambasting for broaching the subject of bringing me to town. I fairly kept my *ladhar* out of it; had my own way of getting round my mam, and to antagonize her wasn't part of the plan. Once I knew they wanted me along, that was enough; then by hook or by crook, I'd be on that road the following Friday night.

The evening light was fading, and I'd hung around the village for an hour. Eventually, the Rowe brothers, Mylie and a few others came out of Murphy's pub, and we set off on our bikes for town. The four valiant rebels were, of course, out front in their rightful places: company formation again, and let nobody dare challenge it. Their tails were up: topcoats flapped back either side of saddles, caps low on foreheads to keep from blowing off, and clipped trouser-ends of turned-up Sunday serge flew round on pedals. No heed was given to stones on the road or to avoiding punctures. They ribbed each other.

You must've taken your Beecham's Pill today, Mylie, did you? shouted the lad in Mylie's slipstream.

Ben Rowe, the funny brother, shouted across: It's the gapes Mylie has. He'd want to go see Henry Bell in Waterford: *Bell's tonic never lets a chicken die*.

But the world of chaffing couldn't mask their intent; a foregathering of dogs to maraud sheep. For fellows who'd lived the Troubles, and to whom fighting and marauding were second nature, to become suddenly redundant, even be made *glugars* of, was like house-training wolves to turn them into pompom-wearing poodles. The wild dog will out. They were at a loss for things to do which were of real value, and any job – by way of earning a living these days – had little meaning; it was only a temporary situation. A night-trip to town was the chance for a bit of daring; to feel again that old rush of blood through the body. A chance to show off their metal to mortals who'd never had the least passion for their country, or if they'd had, were too afraid to lift their miserable heads above the parapet. So men of valour, who would go over the top, were indeed a rare breed. Aye!

Going downhill to the Big Bridge crossroads, Mylie and the Rowes braked and held back to let the rest of us go ahead. They were up to something. The reason was round the next bend: two civic guards stood in the middle of the cross. Sergeant Howard and his sidekick, Ryan – ah, our first encounter – stopped us, asked where we were all off to and checked our lamps. What's your name? Ryan says to me, though he probably knew it; anybody connected to the likes of Mylie and the Rowes would have been known to the Peelers.

Eamon de Valera, says I. What's yours? No way was I going to show deference to those bastards.

Get off your bike, you impudent whelp, says he. He was going to lay down the law – not that there was much of it about then. The sergeant came over to stand with his deputy. An idea hit me: a chance to prove something to the others. I got off, like he'd asked. The next thing, I flung the new bike against

Ryan's long scrawny legs, and then threw a hay-maker at the sergeant. My swing missed him, but his didn't: it landed on the side of my gob, and the next thing I was arse over head in the gripe.

Are we having a bit of trouble here? says Ben Rowe. The boys, the cute hoors, had sent us ahead as decoys, so that they could swoop on the goings-on, and leave bikes dropped anywhere on the road, wheels spinning. The third Rowe brother grabbed the notebook from Howard's hands, leafed through it, tore out all the pages in one bundle and handed him back the black cover. The Rowes and Mylie gathered in a circle round Sergeant Howard, at close quarters. Someone from behind knocked the cap off the sergeant, and it bounced into the ditch near me.

Very interesting, says your man, flicking through the loose pages; even though he could neither read nor write. You won't be wanting this now at all, will you? He stuffed the wad down his breast pocket, pulled his greatcoat tight again and knotted the long belt round his waist, ready to move on, business over with – well, almost.

Guard Ryan, who'd stumbled and fallen when I'd thrown the bike at him, was just getting up as Mylie, *moryah*, accidentally stepped on his ankle. I expected to hear the crunch of bone breaking, but all there was was the hissed anguish on the hoor's face. Good on you, brother! Go on, boy, give it to him.

Oh, I'm awfully sorry. Do hope I didn't hurt you,

says Mylie, with a fancy accent as if he were an actor. Brazen as you like, he was, as he bent down to pat your man's shoe. He lifted Ryan's foot ever so gently, patted the shoe again and let it plonk to the ground. No, the foot wasn't broken.

Jim Rowe, who'd taken no part in the caper, came over, reached down and gave me a pull from the ditch. He looked at me and winked, and then rode off towards town. The rest of us followed. Before we rounded the next bend, I looked back to see Sergeant Howard put on his cap and Ryan heck across the road.

Those two need to be taught a bit of manners, says Jim Rowe without turning his head.

Aye, says Mylie, it's a while now since their last lesson. We all knew what he was referring to. Two years before, the previous sergeant had got the blast of a shotgun in the legs; he and the guard with him had refused, though politely asked, to hand over their bikes. After that, when you'd meet a Peeler, the first thing he'd do was check your bike to make sure it wasn't government transport you were using.

Uphill, downhill, over the last hump and into town. Two church spires, Johnny little and Johnny big, were prodding upstairs into the night sky. Of course, to be different, Johnny big had to have narrow butty wings – high up and shaped like the padded shoulders of Kate Kelly's summer frock – though on this night the dark was too low over the town to see them. The previous time I'd been here was to get a sale for my mam's geese at the St. Thomas' Fair, and the spires then were like upside-down icicles against a turquoise heaven. But on this night, it was a town of gas lamps, half-shadows raking across the walls of stepped houses and patches of streets where the shadows were pure black. All downhill: down the Main Street, and left at the hotel into the dark of Irish Street, the usual route for the boys.

They stopped at the door of a man who used to store guns and ammo, and rapped out a three and a two on the cast-iron knocker. The quartermaster, the boys called him. Ah, the hard man Pat, says Jim Rowe when the door opened and a fellow with a head of hair for a moustache appeared from a lit narrow passageway. So much light: it seemed to want to escape past him onto the street, as he stood there in shirtsleeves and waistcoat looking us up and down.

Just bring them on through, says the moustache, referring to our bikes.

Will you be up late? says Jim Rowe to him when we'd finished parking the bikes out the back.

Oh, don't worry, Rowe. The key will be in the usual spot.

The captain followed the quartermaster into the kitchen. But before he disappeared, he turned to us.

You go ahead, lads. I'll see yous over in the square in a few minutes.

Before the door closed, I could hear them talking about war-flour and cheddar. There was an officer kinship between them, to which the rest of us weren't privy. No skin off my nose, but the brothers and Mylie, who'd spilt as much blood as the next fellow, had a right to feel peeved. But if they did, they didn't show it; nothing was said.

Like all countrymen not used to streets and footpaths are supposed to, we stuck our hands down our trousers' pockets and, outdoing each other, did the pendulum walk up to the picture house to see the noticeboard. Ben Rowe mocked his brother who couldn't read, the way he slowly unscrambled the name of a picture, and we chafed hands, laughed and ragged one another. We stepped it out as far as the south wall of the Salthouse Lane off the Mill Park Road; then back by the castle and over by the dance hall to see if the music had started upstairs. We settled for the square; walked round it three times anticlockwise – to kill time, we said – from one door-niche to the next. Eventually, we glued our arses to Tobin's shop sill, the best spot for gawking at women going to the dance. Jim Rowe poked his head round the hotel corner and strutted over to us.

That was a long few minutes, says Mylie, giving him the cut.

What's your bother – didn't I get you these? says

Jim Rowe. He produced four tickets from his breast pocket: club passes for the dance he'd got from Pat the munitions man; one each for himself, Mylie, Ben Rowe and me. The third Rowe brother, along with the other fellows, wanted to go to the pictures.

Time for the dance. Over with us to the Athenaeum, down the hall, handed over our passes and left our overcoats in with the cloakroom attendant. Then up the flights of narrow stairs at the back until we were right beside the stage, looking down onto the dance floor. A band, almost beside us, played music that was like nothing I'd ever heard. The beat was different, not quite reel or jig time, slower and very fluid, and instruments I didn't know the names of then: a piano, double bass, banjo, violin and a piano accordion. The fellow at the drum-kit sat behind the others. And the dancing was strange: men and women stepped in pairs around the great room, like they would for an old-time waltz, but this was faster, more of a trot. The music and the sight of dancing set off a twitch in my stomach; a new world had opened before my eyes. I tucked in behind Mylie and the Rowes: down the steps onto the dance floor to make our way, between couples whizzing round to our left and a line of women in multicoloured dresses seated on our right, towards the back of the hall where the men seemed to be holed out.

And your next dance, please, said a voice from

101

the stage, barely audible over the clamour. The pattern of great circling motion, that a moment earlier had been the dance floor, at once turned to clamour and disorder.

The in-between-dance confusion lasted for a couple of minutes. There in the men's zone at the back of the hall, fellows who had been eyeing up women and lost track of them were on tiptoes stretching their necks to scan. Others who'd stood like statues for the previous dance were at the front, poised for take-off when the band would strike up, as if it were the starting line for the hundred yards dash. Most were going around like headless chickens – 'cept that their heads were on. In the mêlée I'd lost touch with Mylie and the Rowes, and ended up, like a piece of flotsam, over against the back wall. I was looking out through one of the tall windows at the building opposite when the band struck up again.

But out of chaos grew order. I edged my way forward towards the dance area. A man in an off-white suit and pure white Panama was at the front of the stage singing with the band. He was paid little or no heed: the dancing was going full belt in that same pattern again of circular motion. This time a waltz, and the couples swung round and round. A couple you'd spot swinging at a corner would then disappear into the weave, the strange pattern of overlapping paths; in and out and around the whole thing went.

Such order as there was to the dance, uniformity of steps and the single direction in which the crowd moved round the floor, would put you into a trance. Like what comes on while staring for a while over a bridge at the water flowing underneath. It's not the water but everything else that appears to move, and you brace yourself against the sudden jerk as you're about to be flung headlong into a turnhole.

Soon, what spiralled round became less a mass of couples separately trotting out their individual style and steps, and more like a great pulsating beast that had absorbed them all into its body to swell out its own bizarre life. My head tried to resist this notion, but couldn't. The magnificent monster still spiralled and chased its own tail. My eyes drifted up to the ceiling for a moment to escape, but the ghost of the thing was even up there and the ceiling seemed to spin. The music spun, too, with it. Faces looked down at me from the shadows. Among the faces, Kate Kelly's glowered at me, and I felt bad. The voice of your ghost-man in the Panama hat crooned away in the gaslight.

Mellow, the moonlight to shine is beginning.
Close by the window, young Eileen is spinning.
Bent o'er the fire, her blind grandmother sitting,
Crooning and moaning and drowsily knitting.

Merrily, cheerily, noiselessly whirring,
Spins the wheel, rings the wheel, while the
foot's stirring.
Lightly and brightly and airily ringing,
Sounds the sweet voice of the young maiden
singing.

What's the noise that I hear at the window, I
wonder.
'Tis the little birds chirping in the holly-bush
under.
What makes you be shoving and moving your
stool on,
And singing all wrong: that old song of the
Cúileann.

Two middle-aged chuckers-out, mighty big men, were standing over my shoulder keeping an eye on proceedings. One says to the other: He's a good singer, ain't he?

Not a patch on blind Ned Wolahan from Limerick, says the other. I remember the night he brought the house down with 'Skibbereen'. Were you there that night?

No, but I remember him of a fair day, singing 'The Rising of the Moon'. A mighty fiddle player too.

Ah, there was Mylie! He was smiling from ear to ear, staring into some old tassie's eyes, a quare-looking one; probably telling her she was the most beautiful creature under the sun, and giving her a dose of the fancy accent he'd put on for Guard Ryan. Never saw him grin as much. When I tried to attract his attention, he ignored me.

There was Ben Rowe trundling a hefty *gwaul* of red satin along the outside of the flow. He was looking up at her over the frames of his specs, like he was in mortal dread she might suddenly collapse on top of him. He would tell us later her name was Mandy. Ben had a severe problem steering Mandy. The pair was bearing round in my direction like a council steamroller, when the woman suddenly stopped waltzing with him and flounced off to the side where her friends were sitting, back near the men's zone. I followed her and loitered among a group of men standing nearby.

Oh, Lizzie, my heart! says she, straddling her great self on the arm of the seat between her friends. As she stretched with relief and threw back her head, her width almost covered the two girls on the seats under. I don't feel well after that, says she. She wiped her face with a silk handkerchief the colour of her dress and fanned her forehead. Wait till I tell you: wasn't I waltzing away there with one of those fellows from the mountains: the quare hawk with the specs. And didn't he give me a little squeeze. I felt this hard thing poking at me through his trousers. Sure, at first I thought he was only delighted to be dancing with such a handsome woman; then I discovered it was a revolver he had hidden.

How do you know it was a revolver? says one of her friends.

I'm telling you I saw the handle sticking out over his belt, says Mandy.

It wasn't the handle of something else you saw? said the other. They tittered behind their hands. But big Mandy wasn't listening.

Not only are they country *cábógs*, says she, but they have guns as well.

Ben ought to be more careful, I thought. Wouldn't do for it to get out that we were carrying guns; would really put paid to our trips to town, might bring Brogan and the town Peelers after us. But the Rowes, not always the same one, had to carry the Smith and Wesson on Sunday night. Nothing was ever said, but you'd spot the bulge when he'd search his coat for the packet of Players Navy Cut.

It wasn't that they were afraid of townies. When Mylie was in scrapes over women, they were well able to sort things out with a few skelps, and the townies had learned to keep a distance. The threat was from groups of Old Staters and former Regulars – supporters of the Treaty in the civil war – in town like ourselves to strut around and go to the pictures or be let in to a dance. Heaven knows, there was enough spleen around after the Troubles to cause wholesale slaughter should old adversaries cross paths. Yet despite the bitterness, there had been few outbreaks of serious fighting, only the odd skirmish since the ceasefire. Plenty of old lip and half-threats, but jibes and the throwing of shapes seldom were followed through. Seven years of grief and uncertainty had made people sick to the teeth of even the least sign of fighting. And, as bitterness replaced bloodletting, enemies learned to live with a grudging respect for each other. Still, just in case, the boys liked to carry at least one revolver between them.

Ben put his hand on my shoulder. Why aren't you out dancing? says he. Muttered rather than spoke it; he always muttered real fast and it was hard ever to know what he said.

I can't do that trot stuff, says I.

What matter? Get out there and learn.

That was some dancing you were doing there with the big one. I was trying to get him to change tack.

That troop carrier! You'd want insurance to handle her.

Why did she run away from you?

She didn't run, says he. He looked at me suspiciously, wondering how I'd found that out. You see, I drove her so hard she boiled over and had to stop. Wanted to sit on my lap to be nursed, she did.

You were the one that was boiling, says I, trying to

107

rag him. Look at the sweat on your face. But he was quick with the words.

That isn't sweat – that's steam off her diddies; she had them stuck in my face all the time. Go on, get out there and dance. Come here till I show you. See that little *saulavotcheer* thing there with the knobbly knees?

Where?

In the blue dress, you idiot. She was asking me about you. You'd want to believe him but couldn't. Then I saw who it was: one of big Mandy's friends, a thin awkward-looking thing sitting beside the big one. And he was right, what she had for knees looked like the knots on a shillelagh stick.

Look, says he, I'll ask the big one again if you ask that little thing up to dance.

Fair enough.

So we made a beeline for the two. But as soon as the big one saw Ben coming, she was up and gone like a shot. She's afraid of you, says I. When I looked back at him, he was stooped down while walking behind me.

She's afraid of being arrested for smuggling, says he.

She's afraid of getting her head blown off, more like.

Go on. And he gave me a shove forward. It was too late, I had no choice but to ask the girl to dance. Her raven hair was tied back in two pigtails, and she looked at me with slanty eyes. Not so much as a word, when I asked her; she got up and followed me onto the floor and put out her hand for me to take. I grabbed her hard bony fingers, placed my other hand on her waist and made a mighty take-off.

But it was too quick, somehow; the direction maybe, or too much force on the first step – though I did lead with the left like you're supposed to – or was it simply someone's foot had got in the way? My body lunged forward out of control, and the girl was unable to remove herself in time. A moment later, I was lying on top of her. Her mouth was open, gasping, and her eyes were ready to pop out – the fright of having landed on her back on the floor. All I could do was look into her face and say sorry.

Could you not wait till you had her outside? says Ben Rowe. The girl got to her feet and disappeared.

There were other places, the Foresters' Hall, Redmond Hall and the Goose Club; but the Athenaeum held the best dances. The more often we went stepping it out of a Friday night, the better things got, and eventually I learned how to steer a partner around the floor without falling over her.

One night, I laid eyes on this nice roundy-shaped girl. Don't you just love them spiralling round-shapes of women's flesh? Eventually, I asked her up to dance. Mag 'the Mumps' Brophy wasn't a bad-looking girl: bobbed hair, blue eyes and what a smile, but boy, could she talk.

My name is Maggie Brophy; what's yours? People that know me call me Mag the Mumps. That's because I had them real bad – the mumps, I mean, sorry. Hee hee hee . . . When I was little, you see, I was very sick; nearly died, they tell. Hee hee hee . . . I don't remember. Do you remember when you were little? I remember nothing before I was six, would you believe? I can't even remember yesterday. Imagine that, not being able to remember what happened last night. Oh now I do: Lucy Tobin called – she's my friend, you see, my best friend – and we went to the pictures down the Arches.

You couldn't get a word in edgeways. She was still talking when the band leader said: Next dance please.

Listen, can I see you home? It was the first thing I'd said, when she paused to swallow her spittle and inhale just enough to keep going. Said it unbeknownst to myself, as if to stem her spate of gab. Those blue eyes studied me. She'd stopped talking. There was the hint of a lovely smile – she ought to have smiled more and said less.

I felt her left hand climb a little around my shoulder: the only approval she'd give. That was Mags for you: could talk for ever, but when it came to saying something worthwhile, she had a different language. Though the music had stopped, I kept my hand on her waist, daring her not to remove her hand from my shoulder to affirm her response to my offer, using her language.

Where's the Arches? says I, to get her talking again.

You don't know where the Arches are! You must be a stranger.

The only picture house in this town is up the Salt Lane.

That's it, silly, says she, and she was off yapping goodo. In love, she was, with Rudolph Valentino, wanted to wear Burberry – whatever that was – and to look like Gloria Swanson. Felix the Cat, says I, is my favourite. But would she cop the gibe? Didn't like to say Buster Keaton; it might give the impression of bad taste, but I knew of no other actors' names, or films. The drawback of being from the country: not a clue would you have of the names of pictures and stars, until you'd hear of them from some girl you were trying to sweet-talk. You'd have to play it cute then, and not be seen as a total corncrake. Ought to grow a moustache to look the finished article, like Mylie, and wax the ends till it was like the handlebars of a motorbike. He said women love the old brush: tingles their lips. But could you believe him?

And Mag didn't mind country *cábógs*. We danced it out to the very end, when the band members began to pack up. Then me and Miss Brophy took off with ourselves up Church Street in the half-light from the gas lamp on the corner. Don't choke me, says she, and lifted my arm slightly from around her neck. We stopped for a court in the first alcove we could find, a red-brick doorway opposite the Protestant Church.

Oh look, there's a ghost peeking round the chapel gable, says I for a lark.

Will you stop, says she, feigning a shiver. Anyway, Protestants don't have ghosts.

Oh, indeed they do, and big ones.

Huddled close to the door we were, when a light came on inside in the hallway; so we shuffled off with ourselves. Up the street, we rounded the corner and disappeared up Maguire's Lane, where there were no front doors or street lights to bother us. We no longer needed to be who we were: she could become Gloria Swanson all she liked, and I her Rudy Valentino – if she'd only stop talking. I hoped she wouldn't mind, though, getting her Bilberry, or whatever it was called, a little ruffled.

When I met up with the boys later, I did a jig on the street to show I was delighted with myself. Every bit as good as Mylie then, I was, for shifting women. Himself and his motorbike moustache.

This became the routine of a Friday night, or the odd Sunday night. Park the bikes, walk the streets, go to a dance – whenever Pat the quartermaster would have tickets for us. And, shoulder to shoulder with the young merchants of the town, we'd survey the bits of fluff for a while. Then I'd meet up with Mag and the two of us would spend the rest of the evening together. Leaving her home afterwards wasn't always by way of a walk up Maguire's Lane; a rainy night would put paid to the hope of a court in the dark. She'd have to be brought directly to her door, and all you'd get to take the yen off you would be a quick hault in some alcove along the street.

That Easter Sunday night saw more people than usual around the streets. Another dance on someplace else: the Tennis Club Pavilion maybe, or the Institute. Earlier, Jim Rowe had said to be careful; that the *other crowd* – Old Staters and Regulars – would be there in force, they always went to the nobs' dances. He had advised us – really, he was directing it at me and Mylie – to stay close throughout the night and especially after the dance. When, as he said, those bloody monarchists could be looking for trouble.

It struck me that Philly Kelly might be in town. His family, while not outright Free Staters, had leanings in that direction – they'd have to be a cut above the rest – and he always attended functions, dinners and hunt balls. It wouldn't do to bump into him while I was with Miss Brophy.

It was a quiet night, and I'd forgotten Jim Rowe's

warning. Me and Mag were heading for the dark of Maguire's Lane. We'd just turned the corner from Church Street when we met a group of fellows. Recognized a couple of their faces, but, not wanting to draw their attention, I ignored them. The wrong thing to do.

Well if it isn't the bold Will Byrne, says one.

Too stuck-up, he is, to say hello, says another – they had mischief on their minds, all right. Friends of Philly's, into the bargain; the very people who would've condemned, though not actually've fought, Mylie and the Rowes in the Troubles: big farmers who gorged off the fat of the land.

Aren't you the fellow who's going with Philly Kelly's sister? says the first.

My o' my, doesn't word get around, I says.

Is this Philly's sister? asks the second.

She's surely not. That's a little trollop here from the town, says a voice I didn't recognize. And I felt Mag get tense under the arm I had round her shoulders. And a right good thing she is too, says he; mind you don't get the pox – sorry, measles, or is it mumps? – off her. A chorus of laughter.

Hey, Philly Kelly, come up here a moment, will you? one of them shouted down the street to another group. Mag had pulled away from me. Two of the other group came walking up the street. I recognized Philly's gait. I moved towards Mag, put my arm round her waist to shuffle her towards Kavanagh's corner and the darkness of Maguire's Lane. But we were surrounded.

The next thing, Mag was on the ground: the one who seemed to know her had pushed her. I threw a swipe and he fell. But I felt a dunt on the back of my neck, and I bent over to protect myself. The black shape of a boot I couldn't dodge rose towards my face, and I went to the ground with feet flailing at my back and groin. A weight came down on top of me, and he was trying to get through with punches to my face.

Then I felt the weight lift. Leave him alone, will yous, a voice shouted. It was Philly, and he'd already pulled two of them off me and threatened them, fists to their faces.

But isn't he supposed to be going with your sister? one of them grumbled.

None of your business, says Philly. His hand reached down to help me up.

Get away from me, I grunted, and refused his help. Himself and his outstretched hand! Fucking hero!

The whipcrack of a revolver froze everybody. Down on your knees, all of you, before I blow your heads off. It was Jim Rowe's voice, a cold anger to it that was new to me. None of them defied him, 'cept Philly, and he got the muzzle of the Smith and Wesson rammed to the side of his head for his trouble. On your knees, you imperialist bastard, says Rowe. Philly, head forced sideways, slowly got down.

Amid sore arms, groin-aches and the taste of blood in my mouth, I felt a good deal of titillation at seeing the gun pushed against Philly's head. Wouldn't have minded hearing that whipcrack again to split the bloody night. Would be nice to suck in a fulsome whiff of gunpowder, what must have filled the air in the aftermath of an ambush on Tans or Free Staters and which I'd got from sniffing the barrel of Mylie's rifle. Some sort of hunger inside willed the pulling of that trigger. Wanted to see my first killing: the thug who'd kicked me the most, the one who'd got me on the back of the neck, or . . . even Philly. Maybe, especially Philly.

Get up out of that, says Jim Rowe to me, as he slipped the gun under his trousers belt and buttoned over his coat.

I looked around, but there was no sign of Mag the bloody Mumps.

NINE

The next Sunday, I went walking by the river. Didn't expect to see Kate. If she were to turn up, it would be to give me an earful or to say she wouldn't meet me again. Some surprise then when she popped out from behind a tree, shouting peek-a-boo. She slipped her hand round my arm and fell into step beside me. Obviously Philly hadn't told her of what'd happened, or of the other girl. A cloud lifted. But that didn't mean he wouldn't yet tell her; maybe he hadn't decided one way or the other. There was still a shadow.

I tried to make things good between us. Heeded her chatter more, and I tuned in when she went quiet or laughed. You're in a good mood today, says she. Near where I'd first lifted her up and dangled her over the water's edge, I got the urge to do the same again. Put me down, what are you doing? says she. It was only the second time I'd lifted her like that, and the suddenness of the movement frightened her a little. This *taom* then came over me: a mad temptation to dump Kate into the river, and show her the gall that was inside me over the Friday night. Her laced shoe somehow fell off. I plonked her on the bank, waded into the river and recovered the shoe before it floated away. We dried it with our handkerchiefs, and laughed at the good of it. The *taom* had gone.

I thought she'd be angry, but it was the opposite: she became more playful in an eager-to-please way, and giggled a lot. But this manner of hers sort of irked me: odd, it wasn't part of her charm. I would've preferred it were she instead to've been more ... put out, haughty like a town girl. It might've spiced things up nicely.

Then it hit me. Maybe Kate knew about Friday night. That Philly had told, but she'd steeled herself to put up with knowing; that she bore her pangs of uncertainty in silence in order to save our liaison. Maybe that's why she was doing so much fawning: driven by the depth of her attachment to me, while at the same time she was simmering with rage, ready to clatter me.

The next Friday evening came. I told Mylie the back axle of my bike wasn't working right and I wouldn't be heading to town that night.

A new bike, what's wrong with it? says he. Take it back. As if he cared.

Birds on the move and evenings getting bright would put a spurt under you, make you look to the future. The thing to do was take the bull by the horns. So after supper I went up the far hill to Kellys'. I'd face up to Philly; ask him how he was after what'd happened in town – it might show some concern. Give him the impression that, at worst, it was a mistake I'd made the previous Friday night. Or a misunderstanding? Yeah, that was it: the whole incident had been confused – an error his friends had made. I could've been there waiting with the girl Jim Rowe was taking home while he'd gone to relieve himself. Without quite putting it in so many words, I might lead Philly to conclude that this was what'd happened. And as well as that, wouldn't he see for himself that I wasn't shaping up for town that night?

I looked for signs on Philly's face when I went in, said hello and mustered a mighty smile of observance, for effect. He returned the smile, almost beamed as if he were delighted to see me and nothing had happened; a peculiar understanding, a priest-like compassion, about him. The damned fellow had such winning ways, what smiling benevolence. Cha Cha was there again. He sat legs out, barefoot in front of the fire, toasting his white toes, crooked black nails, to the flickering embers on a half-burned baulk of ash, like he owned the place. His head turned when I entered, and his eyes followed me.

Nanny Kelly gave the fanners' wheel a sudden twirl; a flurry of sparks and dust rose to attack your man's feet. He squealed like a cut pig and fell backwards off the small stool. The sudden unreality, that grotesque thing on its back on the floor with its feet up flailing the air, turned the kitchen into a circus tent. Philly laughed and pointed at his mother: She's been hankering for ages to do that. Indeed, her face had a smug look. I laughed because Philly was laughing. A pair of eyes by the flagstone stared at me, a strip-teethed leer to his face, but I dodged his mockery. Instead, I looked away, cursed him and sniggered all the louder, in defiance. The clown kept the act going, continued kicking his feet and feigned terrible pain, as the laughter rose like shrieks in a charnel house. An end to scoffing; that bastard was asking for trouble. He'd get it too, but not there, not in front of that lot.

Get up out of that, you big oaf you, says Nanny.

She gave him a thwack on the arse with the coal shovel she'd plucked from behind the fanners. Though never the one for skitting much, she played such a foil-to-the-fool act, she could no longer keep a straight face herself. The old scalder probably savoured her own performance the most. She put her hand over her mouth and tittered like a schoolgirl. Uncanny though the farce was, it wasn't unpleasant to see Nanny that way. Would remind you of previous times, when Philly and I were going to school.

If you'd wanted smoky rashers, says the clown, I'd have brought them from the shop.

More laughter. He got up, brushed himself down, put on his socks and boots and made for the door.

I'd better get out of here before the woman murders me, says he.

Nanny feigned a downward skelp with the shovel onto the stool where he'd been sitting. I ignored him as he again stared at me. He turned to Nanny.

Where's Kate? I haven't seen her all evening. You know you'd want to keep a better eye to that daughter of yours; there might be any breed of mongrel sniffing round the place.

Philly got up and made after him.

Plants himself down on the hearth like a pig in a pen, every time he comes here. Has he no fire in his own grate? Nanny gave out to the silent, black figure in the soot corner. No harm, though, to what she was saying; it was just by way of putting a finishing touch to the farce that had gone before.

Hello, stranger, says she then. At last, it was acknowledged that I was there. Blood flowing and her tongue already sharpened, she shifted her broad beam on the seat and set her sights on me. It was time to be off. Any excuse: I muttered something about wanting to talk to Philly. And I slipped out of the kitchen, but lingered for a few seconds in the porch. Nanny probably thought I'd gone – though she could easily have checked through the spy-hole behind Pat's head.

I don't like that young *sleedar* around the place, says she. I'd be afraid he'd have his eye on Kate.

I no longer doubted where I stood with that old *pusthoge* of a hag. Just her nature to look down on the likes of me and all belonging to me. That's the way things were, and it hit home. I'd never get approval to walk out with Kate.

But when he has nothing else, a fellow has his pride. My line was every bit as good as hers. I was proud of my brother, his effort in the struggle for independence – what I too would've been part of, had it continued. My crowd was better, if all truth be told. And if my father'd had a bit of land under him, too, who knows, he might've lived longer. At least he, or his father's people before him, hadn't stooped to become land-grabbers. Nanny had her few acres because old Kelly, Pat's grandfather, had stepped in after the eviction of the previous tenant who'd failed to pay a rack-rent. Only on the back of someone else's hardship could this old harpy set out her stall. But she wasn't going to gloat over me. And if the chance ever arose, she'd be let know in double-quick time what her rudiments were.

For the moment, though, a different tack was

called for. To win over Philly's confidence, I'd again have to become a regular caller to the house. Getting his trust back was as pressing a need as I had to be with Kate.

I followed Philly and Cha Cha down the road from Kellys'. Philly was going to the village to meet Maysie Dunne – huh, such loyalty! And welcome to her he was too. That dead-head flower! Far from growing into the woman we'd expected, or anything near that, her cheeks had gone from cherubic to chubby, and those once-appealing legs had merely filled out into no particular shape; though her hair and eyes did retain their lusciousness.

It's not to say she still didn't have something of an aura. If that's what you like: the overripe fruits of September, second blooms on roses and strong aromas of autumnal . . . decay maybe. Things in their last hurrah. Mylie was a devil for this – the fondness he had for decadence. Take those plump, older women at the dances. He didn't have to be so crude, though, the way he put it when anyone ribbed him about it; we all knew what he meant. Was that what Philly saw in Maysie: a rich, overfed remnant of brown beauty? By then they were as enduring as any married couple. All a bit stifling I thought really.

On the other hand . . . well, it's not easy to blacken out memories, or the strange body-stirrings that go with them. Even after all the years, you'd wonder what it was exactly those two got up to when they were together – hardly playing toss-the-ball yet, while standing in their nip? – and what had she got that kept him from losing interest. Such a curiosity would gnaw at you.

Philly and Cha Cha were well down the hill when I saw them ahead. Take your time, Philly, old son, will you? I called. They stopped. I have this hurl nearly shaped out I'd like you to see – might suit you. Are you going to the village? Of course he was going to the village. Takes effort to make conversation when your enthusiasm runs against the grain. Why don't you come up to the house when you're passing our lane and see it for yourself?

Hurling was second only to music in Philly's interests. And like anything else he ever put a hand to, he mastered it so damned easily. Nature's child. The rest of us mortals had to strive with each step of every undertaking. But shouldn't I have counted myself lucky: was I not the maker of tools, craftsman to the artist?

For everyone said Philly was an artist with the hurl. Were it not for circumstances, no doubt but he'd've been on that team of '26 and '27. That band of mighty men. But in 1924, who was to know what the future had in store? I brought him over to the workshop. He ran his hand down the grain of the hurl, gently following each curve, like he was in touch with the inner being of wood: what it could do, how far it could send a leather *sliothar*. Shaped from a plank left for a year to dry, then planed and shaved, it still needed a shaving here and there and a good sanding to be just right.

The moment Philly laid eyes on it, he wanted that stick. How much will it set me back? says he. I didn't reply – hold the moment and savour the experience. Well? says he.

I knew he was hooked. Wait, weigh up the reply for the exact dose of effect. I'll tell you what – hold it there, just a moment's pause, and – you teach me the accordion and you can have the weapon with my blessing. But you'll have to wait till it's finished.

Is that possible?

Is what possible?

Teach you the accordion?

Oh, he was smart all right, the hoor. Cha Cha, taking it all in till then, started to laugh, belly-laugh – belly-shake. He jigged his head to some tune or other and, in blatant mockery, his hands played an invisible accordion.

Music lessons from Philly was not what I'd wanted, and not what I tried to get across. A gesture was all, a mere token, in return for presenting him with this item of pure craft; and for considering that he alone was worthy of such a stick – a lesser quality one would have done him. Why had I bothered? Was my acknowledgement of his skill not enough, that, into the bargain, he had to scoff?

Little I could do 'cept laugh it off with them.
Lessen their mockery by mocking myself. I suppose,
says I, you can't teach dogs to fly. I was about to say
pigs, not dogs, but I didn't want to fawn too much,
or show that I'd lost my self-possession. But this
was another slip.

You mean teach old dogs new tricks? says Philly.
Or did you mean, says he: pigs will fly before you
learn the accordion?

The cheek of the hoor! And not a side of him I'd
seen much of before.

Frying frigging pigs! says the lug after him, bend-
ing down and slapping his knees at the good of it.

Cha, I said flying pigs, not frying. Philly let on to
be pontificating like Father Cormick. The lug
hopped around the yard, snorted and flapped his
arms. Philly was beside himself laughing.

Mylie, who had been inside the door listening to
the racket, came out when he saw his chance,
sneaked up behind your man and gave him a kick
up the arse. The lug went headlong into the ducks'
dung-lough. But there was no stopping him. He got
to his feet, hopped around and flapped his arms
worse than before.

Mylie enjoyed the show. A strange caper – more
bizarre than funny. All antics, no wit, and none of
that sense of fun that real wit gives you. At best, it
was another crude circus show where the spectators

roared at the bawdy antics of a fat, wet clown. The hideous spectacle didn't last long, thank heavens; for who knows what barbarity might've come about.

Mylie, with his good clothes on, got his bike and walked with us to the village. He was going to meet the Rowes and head for a dance in town. I had the urge to change my plans and go with him. He told Philly he'd heard that Kellys' were going to hold a ceilidh, that Philly and Cha were supposed to be getting the tunes together.

Is that right? says he. Or is it only a rumour?

Philly said they might be, but he didn't want word getting round, not just yet till preparations were more under way. I hadn't heard anything of this. But the worm inside was made worse a few minutes later, when we rounded the next bend in the road.

I hardly minded them at first. It was only natural he should walk with her, if they were going the road at the same time. He'd have known her from going in and out of the shop. No need for undue concern, when I saw them in the distance strolling towards us. She moved along the soft margin of the road, while he walked the stony cart-rut nearest her. I recognized his scrawny legs, made all the more gaunt by the way bicycle clips held the trousers tight to his thin ankles. Could picture him from the evening, arse on the ground and pain on his face; Mylie had landed on his foot. She wore that lovely grey-green tweed coat over the repp costume she'd got for forty-five shillings in The Hibernian House's summer sale in town the previous July.

I still didn't set much store by it, when Cha, half watching me, shouted: Look, don't they make a lovely pair? Doesn't it do your heart good, says he, to see the birds, bees and children of the fields get together to propagate. Ah, I can smell spring in the air. He cocked his nose to sniff. Nothing the lug might say to grig me would make a difference. Impossible to think that Kate would find Guard Ryan handsome; he didn't have enough flesh on him to tickle her fancy. What concerned me was if Mylie, when he had an audience, might have another go at the Peeler. Not that I was worried for Ryan; I just didn't want a scene in front of Kate.

When we met, Cha made a big fuss of Kate, and Philly chatted to Ryan. Mylie walked ahead, and fixed his trouser clips to get on the bike; I stood with him, slightly away from the others. Kate, as I expected, came over to me. Mylie got on his bike to push against the hill, the back wheel filliping out road pebbles behind. Kate wasn't the least put out that I'd come across her walking with a fellow.

Didn't expect to meet you, says she. What are you doing around these parts of a Friday night?

It wasn't like her to probe there and then; not even when we were alone, 'cept in fun, but this wasn't in fun. You'd think my meeting her this way would've had a different effect on her. Her cheeks ought to've turned red, or at least blushed; she should've felt awkward, the way she'd done that time she landed in her mother's kitchen to find me there before her. Most of all, I should've been able to read the secret signs, like I could that time before. But here she had a new set of signals which was beyond me. What was she doing associating with bony-arse here while my back was turned?

What difference does it make? I snapped. You hardly need me for company.

Surely you're not jealous of me talking to Joe? Really! She had a slight grin that taunted. Sharp as a vixen, with a vixen's insight to my innards. There's really no need to be jealous, says she. Her grin mellowed to a soft smile, but the satisfaction wouldn't leave her face. A trait inherited from her mother, no doubt, which seemed to say: I know things about you, secret things, and I'm going to put my fingers round those chicken-livered bits of your insides to make you squirm.

Joe, she'd called him; never knew his name was Joe, or even that he'd had one other than Guard Ryan.

So it's Joe is it? says I. Felt my throat tighten; like when her brother had stolen the girl on me in school. But steady on there; that excuse for a Peeler isn't even trotting after you when it comes to the ladies. Stop worrying, and fix your mind on a town full of willing pullets.

I kept looking back as the two of them walked on down the road, their shapes and manner towards each other chiselled into my brain. Did I, at one point, see him slip his arm round her? Couldn't be certain from that distance in the fading light. Some sort of recoil spring inside my head was being pulled back. The lug was watching me, probably Philly too, but I was beyond appearing touchy about what they thought. Still and all, the spring wasn't fully recoiled. Not yet.

TEN

Simon

Met a bloke down the pub the other night, who'd only just come over. It turned out he knew my wife's people – Nora is from Galway. Like everybody, it seems, from that neck of the woods, he was a musician. He carried a fiddle, and we ended up doing a session.

At sixteen, I took to the music again. Cha called to where I was working, that place on the hill where the old lad used to visit – if visiting is what you'd call his antics. I'd gone working on the farm for the woman there, Kate Kelly, when I left off school. A bit of a slog at first, but you'd get used to it. As a boss, she was exacting, but otherwise treated me with respect. You might say she had a certain regard for my welfare; encouraged me, she did, to be interested in things other than work.

Cha walked right in on what I was doing,

131

pronging dung from a pighouse, and asked me to go with him and play for a house-dance, across the mountain in the next county. The Kelly woman took no exception to my having to leave work early. In fact, it seemed like she too might go along, she was that excited about the night ahead.

Make sure you wash the pigs' smell from under your nails, says she, and came out to the gate to see us off.

She's a strange one, I said to Cha, as we headed across the White Mountain. One minute she's strict, the next she's nice as pie.

I'll not have you say a bad word against that woman, says he. A lady if ever there was one. There's more to her than you're ever likely to know.

I wasn't running her down, I said.

Well then don't, he snapped. And we spoke little for the rest of the journey. A right dazzler she must've been in her day: at least two geezers, that I could count anyway, were keen on her – pardon me, one of them was only keen on her hayshed. Not a blooming sound as we tramped along; only the constant brush of damp heather against our trousers, and the thump thump of Cha's big feet off the soft turf. What a pair of feet he had.

A fair old hike it was, too, across the hill before dark, with the accordions in wooden boxes that Cha'd made strapped to our backs like knapsacks. Through a heavy mountain mist, we had to be careful on the narrow sheep-tracks, criss-cross, in and out: must've been twice the journey the crow flies. Eventually, we dropped into this mud track leading to a place farther down, and came upon the dwelling-house from the rear. Bare stone walls with a roof pitched like a church roof, yet so squat that we were above eaves level at only twenty yards away. We shambled down the steep bank by the gable so as not to fall, and turned in a U-shape to face the front. No porch: a wide open door into the kitchen, as if the inside were an extension of the outside. Light from three wall lamps and two hurricane lamps swaying from the ceiling and young ladies, at least five of them sitting on a form by the far wall, were sudden to the eye. Pure delight and a jolt to the system, you might say, after an evening's trot over a stark mountain. The shapes to the girls' bright soft legs were appealing in the light.

A wireless rested in the window niche by the stairs inside the front wall; its open back faced out to reveal its all. The most obvious bits, a light-blue dry battery and the softer – ouh, soft as those girls' legs – lines of the wet battery blurring with the glass valves made up an apparatus that was strange and too modern by half for such a place. The heads of three men bent over the wooden box. An aerial raked up to a white insulator tied to the metal chute at the eaves, over to a makeshift pole high on the embankment we'd just come down, round another insulator and off to a tree in the field beyond; and then into the ether. There was definitely more there than your usual hundred feet of aerial. The earth-wire came out through a hole in the bottom sash, and down to a steel rod in the ground. Like a blooming post office, it was, with all the wires. One of the heads inside the window lifted and looked at us crossing the yard, the mouth moved but the other heads didn't look up; they were too absorbed. Lord Haw-Haw's voice – *Germany calling, Germany calling* – came over the radio crackle, and three intent faces, inside a window, are as burned into my brain as the tongue Cha'd spoken about when I was a child.

When we landed on the kitchen floor, one of the girls jumped up from the form and threw her arms about Cha's neck, like she was his sweetheart; though she wasn't. Full of the joys she was, brown eyes, dark hair and wiry, skinny legs; and as wild as the place roundabout where she lived. Hello, Uncle Cha, so long since I've seen you. Another girl, probably her sister, came over and hugged him, less enthusiastically, but she had more style and allure. Though this one didn't look so wild, there was a glint in her eye and a lingering to that hug that belied her outward manner. An attractive, simmering bit of stuff: too dangerous to handle – for a young fellow anyway. Oh boy! Eyed me up and all, she did, but decided she wasn't going to squander what she had on a sixteen-year-old. After a plate of bacon sambos and tea – so much tea: no signs of rationing there in '43 – it was down to business, and on with the music.

Jigs and reels, it was, for the rest of the night, till well into the early hours. Apart from Cha and me there was a piper from Waterford. Met the same bloke a couple of years later in Cricklewood, but he didn't remember the night. I've played in so many places, says he, I can't recall.

Kate Kelly has written to me a lot in latter years, and occasionally I'd reply. Her first letter was the surprise. What's this now? I says, when I check the name at the end before reading the letter. How did she get my address, and why is she writing? Probably wants me to remember a barley mixture we once fed to winter stock, or trawl half London for some apothecary selling an animal drench she's seen in a journal. But she wasn't asking for anything; just went on about how things were on the farm, how my folks were doing, and that was it. Peculiar? Very peculiar. Within six months, she'd written again. And this time I replied; felt I had to.

She was lonely, I reckoned, getting on in years, with not a lot of people round there she'd feel comfortable talking to. So what does she do? Ups and writes to muggins here, that's what, her one-time slave about the yard. Strangely enough, it's easier to talk to someone who is far off, not living in your hair. Like striking up a conversation with a stranger in the pub: you end up having a long chat. Beats sitting at home looking at the wife, the two of you having said everything there is to say.

When I wrote back to her, the few times I did, it was a lot easier to tell her things about myself than when writing to my mum. Practical things – she was a practical sort of person – about work: the makes of tractors and drag-lines I'd operated on various sites round the city, and the latest digger, back-acter type, I'd seen in the firm's yard. Told her about the area I lived in and my house, didn't say I didn't own it – didn't say that I did own it either. Not very good at divulging personal things. If she wanted such news, she ought to chat to my mum: a curiosity for them to have in common – might make friends of them.

In her last letter, Kate Kelly asked me if I still had an interest in farming, if I'd ever considered moving back home, or if I'd become too used to city life? Now that's what you might call personal, a bit too personal coming from someone outside my immediate family. And too close to the bone; you just don't ever let yourself think about going back. Of course, I tell the mates I will, when I get the shillings together. But joking aside, to harbour such notions would only interfere with your life, fill your head with nonsense. As it is, there are enough zombies going about, dreaming of the old sod they ought never to have left. Gotta take life here by the scruff of the neck.

So in my next letter, which wasn't written for some time, I fobbed her off with a few general remarks. Not that I ignored the matter completely. Not much point going home, I wrote; it wouldn't be very practical. In the one cottage with my parents! And what chance of supporting a family on such poor wages? – couldn't resist a dig at the pittance she'd once paid me. And polite enough to her, I was. Though the urge was to write: Well, Miss Kelly, what business is it of yours what I intend doing in the future? It ain't no skin off your nose.

ELEVEN

Ah, there it is at last: the picture gets clearer and the music rises. So I've found them, my ghosts, or is it the other way round? The table is gone from the floor, and forms are pushed in by the wall. Here they come in pairs, feet flicking out from the shadows, as if they've been dancing away for ages while it's only now that I've broken in on them – or maybe it is they who've allowed me in: no longer possible to tell which, and it really doesn't matter.

There's something different about this night; can feel it in my bones. The old pair are gone from their chimney corners, thank heaven: no gawping eyes to put a damper on things. The fire blazes under a griddle hanging from a pot-hook; I love the smell of rashers and blood puddings. The voracious hunger we all have. Kellys' biggest kettle is on the next pot-hook, just off-centre of the main flames rising, but still manages to blow steam.

Yes, that's what's different about tonight: the insatiable hunger in the air – greater than what food can appease. Each of us young ones has the worm inside, to drive us beyond the beyonds in doing whatever it is we're going to do. Wild. The dancing, you can tell, will be non-stop, head-to-head chats between friends tonight will turn to fighting talk, words will turn to deeds. Impulses between men and women will be satisfied – either through groping indecently in the porch, behind the parlour door or in the secrecy of the shed, on the soft hay. Moments stolen from ordinary time.

Together, Philly Kelly and Maysie Dunne come in through the porch, into the light. The tell-tale looks they give each other: they've already satisfied their urges. Just couldn't wait, could they? To lay eyes on her causes a yen in me – who's the clown who says time heals?

The music tonight will be mightier than ever. Cha and anyone who ever played an instrument here is here again; already there's a fullness of sound. Philly, too – when he's ready, that is – will strap on his instrument and join them.

Neah, ded diddley a, diddley aten naten yaa,
Da ded diddley a, diddley aten naten naa . . .

A flute and fiddle are countered by accordion

basses, and also by another sound: drones and chanter. Yes, there's a set of pipes here tonight. When in full swing, it lords it over all the other instruments; the organ of the night can hum from a point higher than where the fiddle apes the skylarks that hover above the Blackstairs and twitter at the dawn, while its crying chanter gets to you like a newborn in hunger – such demands.

The musicians, before now, have come to terms with each other's different versions of the same tune. They've ironed out discords not through speaking but by the twitch of a forehead, a cock of the head or a half-glance at the dissonant instrument; though mainly through that odd intuitive knowing all musicians have. And have managed to produce this sound, this magic. As always, despite their talents, their role is a secondary one.

It's the dancing that matters, and dancers are the stars, always the stars. This time it's an eight-hand reel. Four couples, the woman to the right of her partner, face each other in a ring. My brother, Mylie, turns his head to look into his partner's eyes and flashes his teeth at her. She's a mighty woman; he always goes for the big, older woman. He catches her fingers between his two hands and gives them a gentle rub, like you'd pat a dog for giving you its paw. Each pair turns right and they all dance once round the ring. Partners sidestep away from each other, men behind the women, and link up with

other partners to swing each other round, then
return to their original partners. As if glad to be
back, they swing round again. The men skip across
through the centre of the circle to dance with the
women opposite. Like an eddy in a river, they
change positions without ever straying outside the
ring formation.

When the set finishes, the musicians stand up,
unbuckle and place their instruments behind them
on the stools. Each goes to the wooden crate on the
dresser, takes a bottle, a black man, uncorks it and
heads outside to suck in the night air.

The dancing, though, doesn't end. Old Jigger
Nowlan, the smith, calls the next set, and four new
pairs emerge from the dark, ready. A powerful man
once, he stands up, clears his throat and starts
lilting – still has a good voice. After a few bars, the
fresh dancers kick in. The clacking of heels and toes
off the flagstone over the horse's head responds to
the voice, and the jigging voice adjusts itself to the
rhythm demanded; so voice and dancers marry in
the primal, pure rite. There are no other sounds, the
way it ought to be. You can almost see the line of flow:
lilter's voice to dancer's ear to dancer's feet. There's an
intensity of old to it; not perfect, but immaculate, like
the fervour in a child's face; and for a short spell it
seems nothing has changed since the start of time.

Then I see them, for the first time tonight. Look,
the tall couple on the right. She is short-sleeved in

her speckled blue frock, and her eyes sparkle. Ryan, in his blue shirt folded to the elbows, looks handsome. It's nice to see a couple happy. But this couple happy! Though why should I care? I can always get on my bike, head for town and search out Mag with the bobbed hair, or scan a dance hall there for some other sweet Mag; plenty of Mags in these parts, too. And I'm hardly bereft of skill in that department.

Kate smiles. I know that smile, and the glow that courses through Ryan's veins now because of it. Such desires. And where does he expect to run those Peeler-pencil fingers of his before the night's out? That object of desire does not belong to you, you bastard; it's my patch you're occupying. I'll sort you out. But wait; must wait.

I see eyes peering in the window, Peeler-friendly faces leering, noses against the glass savouring the goings-on. They look at me and their smiles move to scorn. They know all right; musicians have that intuition. Nothing surer than they're out there commenting on and relishing the spectacle, like they themselves planned it – who's to say they haven't? Get back in here, yous wasters. Get on with the music; take that other caterwauler to hell out of there. And like obedient children, that's exactly what they do: come in, strap on their instruments and begin to play. But instead of music, the accursed pipes continue with the same yelping that Tom the Jig was making. Am I condemned for life to hear nothing but wailing and caterwauling? And there too, listen. Someone is sobbing in the dark, or is it my head playing tricks?

Why am I stuck here in the shadows, with leering faces all about, while the grand couple is over there in light that's brighter than that from a burning oil lamp? And the music of earlier comes back into its own: the whining pipe-reeds compete with the crying chanter, as Philly's right hand outplays his left and Cha, the clown, fingers his whistle into a lilt of notes that, at the same time, are both piercing and sweet. Then something else happens to the music, and it's the accordionist who makes it happen.

It starts with the second part to the jig. Philly glances at the other players, gives his accordion an extra outward jerk to draw in more air and brings the tune to a higher key. The others respond to the challenge and rise with him, a fraction of a second behind, though scarcely noticeable. Then perfectly on the beat and without hesitation, they begin St Anne's Reel. The world becomes enchanted, with this kitchen its vortex – the river eddy that draws all flotsam to its core, and then under. And like a river quickly in flood, the mood of enchantment rises till we're all delirious. Though brought about by the players, it is inspired by him; first and foremost, it's Philly's creation. The harmony between the instruments, despite the frenetic pace, is magical enough to bewitch the night. A ghostly thing. The dancers have to stop. Even those of us with scarcely a note in our heads, or who've never in our lives tapped exact time, stop chatting. People recognize greatness, its rarity, when it comes amongst them, and know when to shut up; that all words are out of place. Bliss reigns supreme now. It's like we've gone to the afterlife which Father Cormick promises off the pulpit, if we're good enough, the way children are promised sweets to be good. But the musicians decide to change the magic; to focus its presence in one direction, as if somehow they've got either the power or the right. At once, there's an air of change.

Now, for some reason, they play for only one couple, while the dancing of the others seems to matter not a jot. That's not fair, not fair at all. The brightness of sunlight falls on this couple, and they shine like stars. An explosion of stars into pairs must have taken place in the night sky, after which one pair landed here on this floor. But not for long more will they sparkle; I'll make certain of that.

As the night passes, the dancing frenzy eases. Out here now in Kellys' front yard, the glow from the window hangs near to the house, as dark closes in good and tight. A summer moon has long since finished traipsing its low arc across the southern sky. The air is still warm though, hot like the unsaid passions and notions of passions left in some people's bodies. Nearly as many couples outside now as inside. I can easily make out Mylie's shape:

his hands catch what light there is, as they go up and down that big woman's body.

Two tall shadows come out through the porch, turn left and walk away together, past the kitchen window – that seems to have my name on it. The light gives them away – as if I don't already know who they are or what's on their minds. Out with them to the haggard beyond, and I follow; but they move faster than me. Maybe they know I'm after them. Away down the haggard they go, and disappear into the jet black of the hayshed; that monstrous thing on four legs swallows them up so that I can't see.

I try to steal in after them, but I'm held back: prevented from moving a step by some force. Can't overcome this vice-like hold. It's stronger than any being – for no man alive can hold me in a rage. The grip round my body is tightening, the air is being squeezed from my lungs and it's hard to breathe; can't even gasp. I cry out to be set free, several times.

Suddenly, I'm awake in my bed, sitting up. Can hear the tail end of my shouts in the dark, as though the walls have echoed them and the whole episode had happened here in the room. Still feel the tightening in my lungs and dryness in my throat. Something of what happened long ago must have repeated itself again tonight. Am I going fucking mad?

There's a stirring in the other room. Must have

awoken her too. Hope she didn't hear me shouting in my sleep: don't want to give her the satisfaction of thinking I might be in pain. What made me say that? I'm not in pain; it was only a dream. These things occurred many years ago, in a different world.

TWELVE

What happened between Kate and Ryan was no more than a fling, a thing or nothing. They weren't a bit suited. It was all only a bit of trickery to take me down a peg, even the score for that night in town over a year before. So Philly had given the game away on me? The cur! Didn't I spot the mockery on his gob outside against the glass while the pair danced?

She didn't have the same feelings for that long hoor as she'd had for me. Couldn't've had! She dawdled with him. Like putty, she'd been, in my hands; an instrument rather, between my fingers, which I alone knew the secrets of, and with which only I could play the best tune. She was bound to know as much, and to feel gaps of unfulfilment. She'd have to make up her mind soon though, or *pogue mahone*, I wasn't going to hang about for ever

– hang around for ever, there's a queer one for you. Wait to see whom she might please with her affections! To get rid of Ryan first, though, might help her see sense.

I lay in wait for him in the ditch down the road. To be sure it was Ryan, I'd tied bits of straw to the spokes of his bike, back and front, so that when he'd pick up speed on the hill, they'd flick against the forked frame. An old trick for night-time. Even if he stopped to remove the nuisance, he'd miss a few in the dark.

Only straw, he'd say, not worth fussing about at this hour; especially when a fellow's tired after a great night's dancing, and things. Yes, those lovely long stalks tickling the flesh, he'd say. Such burning in the fingers while touching and lying there on the flat bouncy stuff – a shedful of springy hay: the ecstasy of it. A few more straws in the dark makes no odds, he'd say. Pluck away there, me boys, off the fork, and play a melody to keep reminding me. Let them pluck at my heartstrings, he'd say. Play on, yous beautiful straws; give me more music.

That fellow's tune would be changed. No better man for the job. The spot I'd picked wasn't far enough down the hill to allow him to gather too much speed to go flying by, and was near enough to the house for me to be able to make out shapes against the glow. A person approaching, their eyes still not acquainted with the dark, was unlikely to detect the figure in wait.

He didn't spot me, or the swipe from the hurley. It was less of a swipe, more a hoosh, a blocking tackle, the way a full-back, both hands on his stick, stops a forward from running in on the goalkeeper, with brute force. A lovely blocking tackle; it was so easy, really; should've taken up hurling for a lark, might've even liked it. Ryan and his bike went tumbling across the road, into the other ditch. The front wheel spun freely, spokes and straws going twang like harp strings being plucked. Ah, good Peeler-plucking music: the sweetest sound of the entire night.

His groaning told me right where he was: dancer's long legs were irresistibly stretched along the road, only waiting to be pulverized. Would that first, though, I could extract their dancing skill, the way essence is got from wild mint, and have it for myself; I'd hop like a butterfly and send my feet to the ceiling at every house-dance from there to Timbuktu – I bucked one and Tim bucked two!

It was one of these very ankles Mylie had stepped on, that evening going to town, and how he must've enjoyed the pained look on your man's face. Because it was dark, I'd have to make do with the cry in his voice. Had our crowd a partiality for feet when it came to dishing out the rough stuff? I found myself lashing down on his ankles and legs with the edge of the hurley. Spasms of energy went through me, and the outlandish satisfaction: such a thrilling pleasure. Exhilarating: the aroma of vengeance inhaled slowly up the nostrils. The wildness of it, that ancestral need to taste a victim's blood and a hunter's urge to finish the job. But wait now. Had to rein myself in: the situation didn't call for that. No point in injuring him beyond repair; not worth the trouble – all that fuss afterwards. Enough pleasure for one night.

He knew what was good for him all right; Ryan didn't show his face at any more dances in Kellys'. Won't swear to it that he didn't meet Kate again on the sly, though I doubt it. I hoped he might guess – but no more than guess, mind – who had waylaid him. Anyway, it was bound to be Mylie who'd come top of the list of suspects; that'd put the wind up Ryan all right.

No clues were left to point to me; I made sure of that. Earlier, before leaving Kellys', I'd let it be known that I needed to be up for work at an untimely hour the next morning; had even told Philly, with the clown beside him listening. Then skipped home, covered myself with an old head-scarf and coat of my mam's, grabbed the hurley I'd intended finishing and giving to Philly the previous year, and returned to wait for Ryan. Had to be careful, though, hanging round and slipping back to Kellys' yard: people were going in and out, couples leaving for the hayshed. Afterwards when I'd given Ryan his medicine, I quickly cleared off home with myself.

I left the hurley in the car-shed, and wondered had it been damaged walloping the legs off your man. Should've thought of that; brought something else instead – an iron bar maybe! So I took down the oil lamp from over the workbench, lit it, put the globe back on and waited till it glowed and the shadows danced off the wall. Out of nowhere, white moths flew against the globe. Some found their way over the top and inside the smoked glass, only to end their short lives in a sizzle. The bits of things lay there on the brass rim-vent below the flaming wick, colours darkening as they stiffened. More pilgrims came flicking at the glass, went over the top, like troops from a trench, to join their martyred mates. Feathery, fluffy bodies were soft like the dresses the girls had on at the dance. Such a sad sight: the wilful self-destruction of lovely things over a hunger for light. Those other moths, at the dance, also wanted to be in the light – would they crinkle up too? Every bloody body wanted the bit of light: Kate, the copper Ryan and Philly – especially Philly. But Kate and the copper also liked the dark – oh, now – when it suited their urges. I could've sorted out her urges for her that night, no bother; and his too, permanently.

That freshly cut look of pale ash – how Philly had

seen it that evening – was gone from the hurl. The wood had turned a dark, dirty yellow; the linseed oil and turps mix did that, and had given it a slight heaviness. There's an odd regret when the colour fades from wood and its fragrance goes: it loses a little of its essence. Old Marty Nolan, who'd given me my trade, had felt this way too. Yet after its night's work, there were only slight dints in it, nothing that wouldn't come out with a good sanding.

Philly could wait another while to get his hands on it.

THIRTEEN

Simon

We've got to make a special effort to go out and find new accommodation. This flat is way too small for the four of us; we're actually using the sitting room to sleep in. And besides, the two nippers are at the age now they ought to have a room each. Since there's little point going to the council, we'll have to plod the streets to look for what we need. Not something I relish, mind. The thing is, landlords are all the same: money-grubbers, in the same class as money-lenders. Suppose we've been lucky with the one we got, the lady of the coat, upstairs.

I'm finding out she's got a heart after all. Apparently our daughter, May, has been visiting upstairs. Nora has just told me. It's been going on for some time, but without my knowing. May will be twelve soon, tall for her age, and is doing quite well in school. She reads to the old bird, whose sight is failing – though she can still count money. And in return, she's given May the run of her book collection. Quite a size; I've seen it for myself. So that's where May's been getting all those books she's been reading lately.

Would pay the old doll better to give our girl that spare room above to sleep in, I says to Nora.

And have her put up the rent? says Nora.

Nora's got the measure of the old bird all right. No flies on my wife when it comes to money. I leave it to her to manage that end of things. Every Friday night – sorry, it's Thursday night now: pay day has been changed since the firm installed a new wages system – I hand her the packet. And I think no more about money till the following week. Nora's got it all worked out: rent, paying the bills, the best places to buy groceries and how much we can spend in the pub at the weekend. She's like an accountant. A pity she left school at fourteen.

The next thing you'll be telling me is that little Bob, too, is paying social calls upstairs, I says to Nora.

That's right, says she. He is.

Is what?

He's paying our landlady social calls. And gets paid for it.

What do you mean?

He goes to the shop on messages for her. And brings her back the correct change every time.

Another accountant in the family, I says, to tease her. I think we'll have to look for a reduction in rent for providing all these services.

The landlady wasn't so decent, though, that time I brought the bike home to Bob. A second-hand one I got in return for a favour I did for one of the lads at work. She wouldn't allow Bob to park it in the hallway. Don't wish to see my paintwork scratched, says she. So he has to drag it through the kitchen and out to the back yard every time he uses it, and gets irritated.

Bob, you've no patience, Nora tells him. Like your dad.

Eighteen, I was, when I had to make my own way in this city; didn't know a living soul. But within a month, I was settled in and had met Nora. It was through her brother, actually, who'd worked alongside me on a service trench for water mains, that we met. Pat Connolly had already been here for a year, and knew the ropes. One Saturday he asked me if I'd do him a favour and accompany him that night. He'd got off with some bird he'd been chasing for ages, while his sister, who'd just landed from Galway, had to be taken out for the night also. So would I ever be so kind as to chaperone the new arrival?

Is she good-looking? I says. Little did I know, or I wouldn't've been so complacent with my response.

How do I know? says he: she's my sister. It's up to you to find out.

The minute I laid eyes on her, I was bowled over. She was a stunner – and still is. Quite like the girl back home I'd seen two years before, where I'd gone with Cha to play at a house-dance across the mountain. The attractive simmering girl, with the glint in her eye, that I'd been a little in awe of. Here was another version of the same model; except this girl was even prettier and didn't have the disdain the other one had. No, she didn't show the glint that said: I'm going to tease you no end.

I wanted her all to myself, and instead of going to the film with Pat Connolly and his date, we ambled along the streets and talked a lot. And so it goes, I've been chaperoning my mate's sister ever since. Oh sure, we've had our differences over the years, but nothing's made me regret settling down with this girl. As lucky as a cut cat, I was, that way – still am. And we produced two fine healthy children.

May is quite like her mother. Tall, good-looking and bright as a button. Even her handwriting is like her mother's. Can still picture the writing on the letters I got from Nora the time I went back home for a few days; the shapes of the letters reminded me of the shape of her body – say no more.

It was the only time I've been back in Ireland in fifteen years. Some notion I had to see the old folk before answering the call-up to do National Service.

When the postman called each day with a letter from Nora, my mum would raise the envelope to her nostrils and smile to herself. She found it hard to resist, but she managed to keep quiet. She's probably wondered since about those letters: were they from the same girl as I ended up marrying? I'd like to tell her, but maybe it's better to keep her guessing. It's not like she needs to know, now is it?

Talking about letters, I got another one from Kate Kelly. Thought I'd fobbed her off when she'd asked me about going back to live there. Oh, but she's a persistent lady, I'll give her that. In fact she sent this letter by return. I was taken aback, you might say, by what she had to tell me.

I hoped you'd have a desire to return to this part of the world to live. An old friend of yours, Cha Tobin, told me he thought you were the sort of person who'd never stay too long away from his roots. By the way, he says he misses the music sessions he had with you, especially playing at the house-dances.

I'll be out straight with you, she wrote – a remark to make a person wary. I would like to offer you and your family the opportunity to come over from London and live here. You may not know it, but you are the closest I've got by way of kith and kin, and you showed, while working here, that you had the makings of a farmer in you. And Cha agrees with me on that. There's plenty of room in this house for all of us. We don't have every convenience, but that'll change.

Only three years ago, power and light were installed through the Rural Electrification Scheme, which will allow us to make so many improvements. A well needs to be sunk to supply running water to the house and farm. A washing machine, refrigerator and bathroom-cum-toilet will soon be commonplace inside every farmhouse round here. And so many more conveniences I could name, to improve our standard of living. But for a woman of my age living on her own, they're hardly worth the effort. A young person is what's called for. This place is on the verge of change and cries out for a young man – and his family – to make things happen.

You might like to think about becoming part of all this, to be the one to carry out these changes. When things improve, the country way of life in these parts might make this a good place for yourself and your family to live. The farm, house and all of it would become yours. Please, do give it your earnest consideration.

FOURTEEN

The townland of Springmount sits on a shoulder of the Blackstairs. The last shelf of arable land, it touches vast areas of mountain commons that rise sharply towards the bare rock capping – should've been named the Blue-Blackstairs. A few hundred yards below the village, the townland road forks off the main road, and runs along the edge of the shoulder like the hemstitch of a coat, from which narrow lanes branch and wander up through the townland towards the commons. In summer, nobody notices how near the shoulder's edge the road runs. *Skeochs*, brambles and yellow furze cover things up, softening the mountain harshness. In winter, you can see the locality better for what it is: a place of down-swirling mists, steep-browed fields and stone, raw stone every place.

Nothing comes easy, living on the side of a

mountain. Indeed, it's a full-time job for people to survive off the meagre fields. Little wonder they are frugal, sensible and have no time for nonsense or the petty goings-on that matter so much elsewhere – where people don't have it so harsh and survival isn't quite as hard. Tillage crops, sheep numbers or the weather is the conversation when one Springmount man meets another. Strange then, how they took to hurling? Mountainy men talk about hurling with the same intensity they do when discussing the things they depend upon for a livelihood.

It was in the twenties that the craze for the game got into their blood; then spread like the plague to areas beyond Springmount. Morning, noon and night, the talk was hurling. Mortal enemies of a few years previous became united in their new obsession. All of a sudden, no boy would be seen not carrying a hurl in the evening, or what looked like a hurl. Sides ripped from seed-potato boxes, boughs off trees and even nicked pieces of sheeting had their shapes changed. When *sliothars* were not to be had, tea-twine was tightly wrapped, then glued, around sleeves torn from shirts, with bits of wood and cork for cores. A boy's dream was to grow up and hurl like the men of Springmount. For that same team had become our team and the parish's. In the years '26 and '27, fifteen fellows became mighty men, had a ballad written about them and gave us all a spring to our step.

* * *

By the summer of '26, the stick for Philly was at last finished. Two courses of sanding it took, to give the final touch. A metal band, tea-chest strapping, was fitted to prevent the grain from splitting. But the interest I'd had when I shaped and perfected each curved sweep wasn't there any more; no longer my creation, the thing seemed to have taken on its own identity. I just wanted to be shot of it. Brought it with me to work one morning tied to the crossbar of the bike; so that on my way home, I'd call up to where the fellows were practising in the field and give it to Philly.

It was getting on in the evening when I stopped on Aillenafaha hill to see could I spot them in the field across, that they hadn't gone home. They were there all right, small shapes in the distance across the valley of Achadhbheatha. So I pedalled hard for ten more minutes. Such a place for practice! Getting there was training enough, without having to spend hours chasing a lump of leather. But that's hurlers for you. An affliction surely: this wanting to hold sticks and skelp the daylights out of each other up and down a field.

Instead of climbing the ditch to watch them, I pegged the bike in the gripe to flatten the briars, and sat on the frame, with Philly's stick still tied to the crossbar. I'd wait till they were nearly finished practising, so he wouldn't get used to it too quickly:

161

let him hang on till the next night to satisfy himself. Nice to think I could have some say in the matter.

They were going full belt inside in the field; the sounds told me what was happening. A backs-and-forwards formation. The forwards were intent on scoring, while the backs' job was to prevent that and keep the forwards away from the goalkeeper. This set-up, with play restricted to only half the pitch, was the hardest form of training: a forward had to run twice the normal amount and jostle much more with his opponent, while it was non-stop high alert for each back. And Matt Flynn, the goalkeeper, had to stay sharp.

The discord of sound coming out was unsettling. One ash stick smashed into another, and I ran my forefinger and thumb along the edges of the metal strap of the hurl under me to check it had been fitted tightly. Feet came thudding like horses' hooves in a race, close to the other side of the ditch. Hurls swished through the long grass as if reapers were mowing the headland of a meadow. Pull, somebody said. Get it out of there. A player had the ball. Good man, Ned, that's it, somebody shouted. Then a sharp whip-crack of leather against wood, the sound of Jim Rowe's Smith and Wesson, and hooves cantered back to their positions before the next ball would get pucked in.

Because you didn't watch fellows practising, it didn't mean you had no interest in the game. Had I played it, no doubt I would've enjoyed on sight all those movements and deft touches. But, being outside the circle of players and diehard supporters, I had to wait till afterwards, when a match got talked about, to appreciate its art. Seeing it through other people's eyes, and their reactions, was what made hurling interesting. A moment's conflict from a game, when told right, was like watching a drama unfold on stage, and you'd regret not having seen it for yourself. The action, though gone for ever, would take on an afterglow, like the aura round the head of an old saint in a holy picture. Thrilling to listen to a storyteller point up fellows' movements, turn ordinary play into mighty feats of hurling and mediocre men into giants.

A time came, though – probably a conjunction of the planets in the heavens – when storytellers didn't have to exaggerate. All they had to do was describe hurling exactly the way it was being played, nothing more, nothing less. The day of the men of Springmount had come. A team that could live up to stories told, fulfil our hopes and make us dream – mountainy man and valley man alike – when the 1926 championship ran over to the following year. Again I would depend on the eyes of storytellers.

Sitting there outside the ditch, it was easy to imagine the Springmount men train; all those stories I'd heard were like pictures in my head. Tall robust backs, two skilful centre-field men, and forwards as fast as hares. With each gallop and puck of a ball, I could put a face to the man, and imagine him the way story had it. I preferred to see them that way than stand on the ditch and watch.

Those in the know said Philly was an artist. He could catch a ball travelling at speed and drive it the length of the pitch, and could outrun the best athlete. He could lace an overhead ball better than any man, and read a game to perfection: be in the right place at the right time. Philly's only short-coming was his approach: too easy-going, they said – the true sign of the artist surely? To win a match was scarcely important; the skill of the game, its beauty, mattered more to him. And he was casual about turning up for training. But that only made people take to him all the more – even his bloody quirks stood to benefit him.

The hurlers were still hard at it, though the light was beginning to fade, when I walked down the road to the walled entrance and went into the field. Philly was too involved to notice; so I called him and pointed to the hurl in my hand. He immediately left his position and came over. There you go, I says, and handed him his new hurley. He took it, looked at it, looked at me and ran his hands up and down the boss like it was Maysie Dunne he was fondling. I'd never seen him stuck for words before. It was best to leave it at that, say nothing; so I turned and walked away. The craftsman had supplied the artist with his brushes, as if life's purpose were complete.

I met Maysie at the bridge near the village on my way home. She was hanging around, waiting for Philly. Not quite the luscious big plum she'd been; hard-pressed to hold from becoming overripe. But isn't fruit only at its best, as they say, on the point of decay, when you can smell it in the air? Such sweet enticement! I stopped for a chat – what boy can resist the temptation to rob an orchard? Those urges had softened my manner till I was talking ouchie-couchie to her, like an old crone looking into a pram, her wizened face about to scare the living daylights out of the infant: Ah, the little babby, musha don't be crying, dote; shush, little baby, here let me comfort you. Would that the infant could talk: Get to feck out of my face and stop frightening me with your ugly puss.

Maysie was as innocent as a baby, the way she let me reassure her. I told her that Philly was training so hard lately he didn't have as much time for her as he'd like. I've just come from the hurling field and saw him running, outplaying everybody, says I. But she wasn't so easily placated.

I can't help thinking he doesn't care about me any more, says she. He was supposed to meet me last night, but never turned up. Big tears slipped down Maysie's round cheeks like raindrops on a pane of glass in summer. My o' my, did this girl need comforting.

Of course he cares about you, Maysie, says I. Can't you see they're all so caught up with training, they've hardly time to eat and sleep? It's only a temporary thing, and then he'll have all the time in the world for you. I sounded so bloody sincere, I nearly convinced myself. But I genuinely felt for her; thought I knew something of the loneliness in those big brown eyes that were like cow's eyes.

But then he'll be at the music, says she, and he'll have no time either. They'll be looking for him every night to play that stupid accordion. She was off sobbing sun showers again.

Leaning slantways off the bike, one foot planted on the ground, I levered myself over towards her and placed my arm about her shoulders – Mr Compassion himself. The gesture was genuine enough, but when she leaned her head on my shoulder and flooded her face again, I got other ideas. The night hunter began to smell blood.

Do you remember the good old days we had going to school? I asked. Those days had been far from good; though she'd probably had a right time, with all the fellows after her. Just something to say, as if conversation were a sideshow to indulge in, while we'd steal down the path towards a bit of mutual comfort, if she were willing.

Wouldn't it be great to stay young? says she.

Yeah, it would, surely, says I. But what a worn-out old tune! She hadn't been the sharpest turkey in school either. All looks and that was it. You'd wonder why Philly had stayed the course. But was he beginning to ease off? A break was what he needed; let Maysie have a little break too. What better time for her to start her diversion than right there and then?

Yous have been going together now for ages, says I. Do you remember when you and he started courting? In school if I remember rightly. Me and Philly used to compete to sit beside you for catechism. Bet you didn't know that, did you? He used to put his hand on your leg. Oh, I was watching yous, a pair of divils. Ah, them were the days, says I. Did she remember that I'd got my hand to her knee the odd time too? I suppose she'd forgotten the pecks on the cheek. But all that was ever in that pea-brain of hers was Philly.

They were, weren't they? says Maysie. The summer showers had dried.

Great old times, says I – oh, great fecking times altogether. Having already managed to get off the bike while keeping my hand to her shoulder, I propped the saddle and handlebars against the bridge, right on the line across from where Mylie and the boys, years before, had holed the stonework for explosives. The situation called for delicate handling. Well, here was your man. Wasn't she lucky Mylie and the boys hadn't blown up the bridge – boom – or she'd've had nobody to comfort her?

Listen, says I, you'd better wipe the tear-stains off your face before Philly comes, and not let him see you like that. Come on and we'll sort you out. She took to the idea, and I led her towards the stile at the side of the bridge. It wasn't a proper stile: two short crosspieces half jointed to two stakes, all cut from the one round pole, butted against the end stones of the bridge's parapet.

First over, I turned to help Maysie, but she was already on the top rung – *Ride a cock-horse to Banbury Cross*. Her leg showed from under the loose, flowery skirt. The flesh-coloured stocking and seam curving upwards behind the knee made her limb attractive enough, less stout than I'd expected, or maybe the fading light made it so. Talk about urges! Of course I made a fuss of helping her, in case she'd slip. Didn't want any injury to Philly's precious *fine lady upon a white horse*, now did we? Had to make sure, too, she didn't catch her skirt off anything. Wait now, Maysie, mind your material. The world of concern, a fellow'd be. There was, though, an odd sense of having been over this fence before somehow.

Steady now, Maysie, don't let go the top of the stile till you've both feet on the ground. I guided my old china doll, put my hands to her waist, and down the slope we went to the level ground below. All the time reassuring her with plenty of old blather. The lamb to the slaughter. Mutton, more like.

I hope there are no briars to catch my stockings off, says she. This is only the first wear I've got out of them; the best of Lisle hose from Bolger's inside. They've got the fashion marks on and all, says she. Hose from The Hibernian House! What more could a girl want? If a girl hadn't her hose from The Hibernian House, she was only in the halfpenny place.

Show me, I was about to say. Mind your Lisle hose, I said instead. Take it easy now, Maysie, don't slip, that's it.

Instead of staying in the open space, in full view of anyone who might stop to gawk in over the bridge, I led her past the little waterfall, and up the bank. We stopped behind a clump of bushes: good cover from prying eyes. Now let me sort out those tear-stains, says I. Off with my coat, like a proper gent, to place it on the ground for her to sit on; I got out my handkerchief and went to the water's edge.

It's all right, I'll do it, says she, and she went about taking the wet hankie from my hand.

No, no, sure you can't see the marks on your cheeks. Just relax and we'll have you cleaned up in a jiffy. It must have been the best wipe she'd had since she was a baby: I spent surely ten minutes wiping off stains that weren't there. Over to the stream to wet the hankie, back to daub her puss for a few more minutes, and then over to the water again. It was like she was the shagging Mona Lisa, the going-over she was getting. Had to laugh at the good of it.

Are you not finished yet? says she, eyes closed and mouth pursed up. But she didn't say it harshly. The thing about Maysie in those days: her sharp tongue hadn't begun to show. A softness of manner made her round body all the more voluptuous. I wiped down to the area round her mouth, and saw that she was wearing lipstick, like a Protestant girl. Made her even more exotic; its soft shade blended with her skin tones, so you'd scarcely notice she was wearing it, unless you were as near to her as I was. Some of the pink smeared the hankie, and she trembled a little when my finger touched the edge of her lower lip. Straight away, I was aware of being close to a border: the dividing line, maybe, between the zones of the regular and the intimate. Certain body urges moved me onwards. Steady on now. Better to retreat and approach the border in a different place: test her defences that I might know for sure how things stood. Borders were there to be crossed, or not crossed, as the case might be.

How well do you remember the days going to school? says I. And I placed my arm round her shoulder again, playfully this time. Maysie didn't answer me; she was trying to think, and closed her mouth to swallow. I would think for her. Do you remember when I used to sit beside you for catechism class? says I. The master was as deaf as a poker. He was some boy, wasn't he? I often wondered was he only letting on to be deaf, to see how far we'd go – like what I was doing at that moment.

Oh, he was deaf all right, says she. I can remember some of them times, says she. The trace of a smile made her cheeks more round and gave a hint of the old cherubic dimples. A reminder of how I'd once thought of her as the nicest thing in all creation, who must surely turn into the loveliest woman. Instead, she'd blossomed too early, like a rose in spring. I'd try to get back to how I'd once seen her.

Do you remember the way you used to go into the titters when I'd go at you in the desk? says I. Had never made her laugh like Philly though. I lifted my hand from her shoulder and placed it round her waist and tickled her the way I'd done in catechism class, or rather, the way I imagined Philly had done – man learns from boy. Like this, says I. And with one finger, I gave her a soft poke to test how sensitive she was to the touch. She responded: her body flinched sideways slightly, and she smiled. So I gradually increased the tickling till she almost giggled.

I mean like this, says I. What I used to love most about them old catechism classes was the chance to tickle you. I'd got her going all right, tittering like a young one. Had that border been crossed? Was I no longer in the zone of the regular?

A water hen kicked up a racket somewhere upstream, noising like a guinea hen in a barrel. And I thought of another occasion: the Sunday afternoon me and Kate had first gone walking by the river. How the water splosh-splashing over mini-rapids and round mossy stones had sounded so musical; how warm and alive the trees and bushes had been. Different place, different time – different bloody world. Nothing since had matched it for magic, and nothing would, either. If you could only remake magic. Kate's face flashed before me, blue eyes penetrating, and she had this heavenly smile; the most wonderful apparition emerging from the evening mist. There seemed to be no link whatsoever between what was in my head and what my hands were up to.

Oh, stop, says Maysie.

I will, says I, and tickled her twice as much. Then I placed my hand to the other side of her head and nudged her face round towards me. Her eyes were closed. There was no longer need to think this process out: let things happen by themselves. With one hand glued to the side of her head, the other rose and cupped her chin, my fingers touched her cheeks and then, ever so gently, her lips. It went on like this for a few minutes, with only the faintest hint of objection; though her eyes stayed closed. She was probably thinking of Philly. Not that it bothered me much; let her have her quirky fantasies. I did wonder, however, how she saw him: as a grown-up with big muscles gripping her pulpy flesh, or as a boy in his pelt standing before her and tossing a ball to her? But none of that mattered, the way things were going.

The touch-testing by fingertips routine changed to full-blown caresses, and I put the gob on her. We had, indeed, travelled deep inside the zone of the intimate. Slowly at first, our mouths gradually increased to full rate of activity, and all other times and places were forgotten. We lay back in the grass and let things happen. She was good at the gatchy-ing, too. Mind your Lisle hose, Maysie, my girl.

Again that old water hen – had to be the same one – flapped against water upstream, busy doing what birds did at that hour. The hour when foxes, owls and things start to prowl, and come into their own. Time for the cat mooching about, nosing the earth, to go suddenly still, having spotted something, and then a lightning spring from stillness to land its prey; its tail would flap from side to side off the ground. The blood felt nice and warm in my veins, and I could understand the other prowlers of the night, like we were all a family.

Afterwards, when the charcoal grey of twilight had been replaced by the night, we made our way back by the stream, up the bank to the stile and onto the road above. She said: Thanks for cheering me up; I feel better now. A queer thing to say.

Oh good, I'm glad I was of some service to you, says I. If you ever need cheering up again, you will let me know, won't you? No answer. Would you like me to walk you home? No answer. When I turned towards her, she wasn't there. She'd slipped away in the dark.

FIFTEEN

The next evening, things took a turn for the worse between me and Philly. I had just got off my bike to walk up our lane after landing home from work when he confronted me. He must have been waiting there for ages, and missed his hurling practice into the bargain. No mistaking the intent on his face or the seriousness in his voice. He never took his eyes off me as he walked nearer.

What were you doing with Maysie Dunne last night? Less a question, more an accusation. Is it true what I'm hearing you were up to?

I hadn't covered this angle. It had never crossed my mind that Maysie would tell him. Surely if she'd wanted their courtship to continue – the evening before being just a bit of diversion, meaning nothing – this was the last thing to do. Nobody else had seen us, I was sure. Or had they? Not again: some fat-bellied clown hiding in the ditch watching! But that would've been too much of a coincidence. It had to be Maysie, with her big mouth and a bent motive.

What's that? says I. Little else I could think of to say.

Don't deny it.

Deny what? says I, and screwed up my face to look bewildered. Always the first rule when caught unprepared: plead ignorance. And I'd play for time till I'd get my neck out of the noose. But the attack was so sudden it stunned my brain. He was too furious, anyway, to listen to reason. If I could only figure out how much he knew of what'd happened between me and Maysie. What are you talking about? says I.

You know very well what I'm talking about.

Haven't a clue what you're on about.

Were you with Maysie Dunne last night?

Ah, that was a start, and then an idea hit me. I'd go along with him, answer yes to each question, but at the first accusation that me and Maysie had got up to what he shouldn't know about, I'd deny it outright. Letting on to be hard done by, I'd lambaste the bloody telltale who'd twisted a perfectly innocent chat between old schoolfriends into a scurrilous lie. Such a scandalmonger had to be sick in the head. Yes, this was the course by which I'd wriggle myself out of trouble. But he wasn't willing to be led down that road. His sense of betrayal was too strong, too overpowering. Can't say I blame him really; what have we got if not some loyalty to each other? That Maysie one was too . . . too foreign-looking by half to be trustworthy.

You rode her, didn't you? he shouted. Ah ha, can't beat the bit of straight talking, I always say. There was no answer to that. His mind was made up; no way of avoiding a fight now. So I went to park my bike against the lane ditch, tried to deal with the stomach-twitching and steel myself. Either hand, though tense, was ready to shoot up and ward off his swipe, the expected haymaker from the left or the right; certainly not the thump that rocked my head back on my shoulders. A straight left, and his fist appeared to twist slightly as it landed. He'd caught me by surprise as I was turning round to face him; I staggered back against my bike, knocking it to the ground, and fell on top of it.

Get up, you bastard, says he. You were never anything but a go-by-the-wall.

That remark stung worse than the blow. We'll see who's the go-by-the-wall, I roared. I was just up off my knees when thump again. And this time it was the haymaker I'd first expected. I was on the ground once more. Talk about seeing stars! A rake of moons floated before my eyes.

And here's your bloody hurl, says he. I don't want the poisoned thing. He picked up the stick I'd given him the previous evening and threw it on the ground near me.

Any creature trapped and humiliated will fight back, by whatever means. Me and that hurl were two allies with a common enemy, and as allies we combined against our enemy. Philly, side turned to us, was about to walk away. I grabbed the stick, stood up and pulled down on Philly, with the edge. It missed his head and shoulders, but not his right arm. Got him just above the wrist. You could hear the bone crack. Philly twisted his face in pain, opened his mouth and let out an unmerciful howl.

You broke my arm, you cunt, says he. In reflex, he crossed his other arm under his right arm to support it, and hunched himself up. Sorely tempted, I was, to give him yet more to be indignant about, and settle old scores good and proper.

What did you expect? I sneered. That's what he'd get for assaulting me.

Revenge was made all the more savoury by the tremor in his voice: For heaven's sake do something. Go get the pony and trap, see if Kate is home to take me to O'Neill the bone-setter.

I left him there propping one arm with the other, and to stand with pain on his face.

In the middle of the kitchen floor, Kate and Nanny stood on either side of me as though they were about to frogmarch me off to some holding cell. They demanded to know what was wrong, and when I told them that Philly had to be taken to O'Neill, they wanted to know how badly hurt he was. What was it?

The arm, I said.

Broken?

I'm not sure. Only the bone-setter can tell.

How did it happen?

He got the smack of a hurl. With luck they'd leave it at that, and wouldn't notice any telltale signs of blood on my nose or eye-swelling under the peak of my cap.

I'm tired warning Philly that no good would come of it, says the old one. Every evening he's off killing himself hurling. And now look at him. Could he not just content himself to sit and play his music at night? I warned him. I was right all along.

Ah, Mam, leave it so, will you? says Kate. Now is not the time to clap yourself on the back for being right.

The girl, at least, had sense. Those blue eyes were fierce. Come on, says she to me; let's yoke up the pony.

I'd turned on my heels to follow her out the door, when old Pat stuck his black head out from the shadows of the soot corner. Who hit him? says he. The whites of his eyes were like lamps against the dark, and flashed their blue the way his daughter had done.

He'll tell you himself when he gets home, I said.

He gave a slight twitch of his head, hardly noticeable, away from me, but his eyes didn't lose their fix. He was keen; I'd never noticed it before, as if he understood what'd happened from the marks on my face. It wasn't my fault; it was Philly's own doing, I wanted to shout.

Nanny stood on the floor, hands to her cheeks, showing her age; her feeble way of behaving belied all the impressions of shrewdness I'd ever had of her. Was she even aware, after all the years, that Philly was courting Maysie Dunne? And how would that little snippet of news affect her notions of grandeur, hah? She was to be pitied really.

Kate clacked the latch of the red door to the stable and went in. She sidled, behind the pair of working horses, over to the pony's stall. This separate enclosure was cosier than the horses' open stalls. The pony's parlour, they called it; the Kellys had a special affection for their pony. Iron scraping off iron, as she pulled back the bolt, grated on my nerves; I felt my teeth tighten in their sore gums. The door creaked open. Kate talked to the pony as she put on the winkers. The animal came clip-clopping backwards through the stable door. Kate gripped the bridle ring linking the bit in the pony's mouth like it was all second nature to her. I thought of her with the dog by the river of a Sunday – the way she had with animals! She held the pony, while

I got the tackle off the peg inside the stable door. Having harnessed the animal, we marched single file like a circus parade, out to the haggard. I pulled the trap out from the linnie, and yoked it to the pony. Kate ran back to the house and returned with two tartan rugs, and candles for the lamp-holders on the trap.

You'd better get his heavy coat as well, I said, when she came out – the first words spoken since we'd left the kitchen. She placed her *gwaul* down on the round-about seating, and without so much as a nod, turned on her heels and went back to the house for the coat.

I took the driver's seat by the door at the back, the side nearest the gripe; she sat across from me and off we trotted down the hill. Not being used to it, my hands felt stiff holding the reins. Kate took faint notice – in the past, she'd no doubt have had a right skit at me, but things had come between us. Anyway, it was soon obvious that there was little need for reins: the pony knew the road.

I felt awkward with Kate and the way we sat strange with each other. Thought I might wink and get a smile out of her, like old times, but she didn't notice it when I looked. Well, if she wanted to be like that, it was fine by me. I gave the pony a *click click* and a swish of the reins. Again in a couple of minutes I glanced at her, but her eyes were fixed in a line just sideways from me, as if I wasn't there.

Sorely tempted, I was, to jump out and leave her to it.

The poor victim sat hunched on a stone at the end of our lane, still nursing his arm. Where did that stone come from? I hoped it hadn't been taken from our ditch; it would have to be put back. Feck off and pull ditches down someplace else; you've enough of them yourself, heaven knows. Philly had a coat over his shoulders. A fellow stood beside him with no coat on, and his belly stuck out over his trousers. Had that hoor no shame? Like a bad penny, he always seemed to turn up. Kate hopped out of the trap first; went over, knelt beside her brother and put her arm round his shoulder.

That's what hurling gets you, says Cha, looking at her. Could he not curb his tongue for once? Never marry a fellow that hurls, says he. See what it brings? He wouldn't have a paw left to scrawb you with. The broth of a man like me is what a girl needs, with two good hands. Cha walked over to Kate and shook his belly in her face. See that for culture, says he; that's what you should look for. The fellow got away with too much; though he did manage a smile from Kate. He came over to the trap, put his hand on the backboard, turned to me and threw me this look – if looks could kill.

I got out of the trap to allow the injured hero easy access. The clown and the girl stood on either side of him; you'd think he was going to collapse. There's nothing wrong with his shagging legs, I felt like saying; it's only his arm. When Philly put his boot on the iron step of the trap, Kate adjusted it sideways from the edge – no, the hero wasn't going to be let fall. The two stayed by his sides till he was aboard.

I drove on with the four of us in the trap, the clown beside me. Kate placed a rug over Philly, who scarcely raised an eye from his own concerns. He mooned for the entire journey: into the village, up through the mountain gap, then uphill downhill all the twelve statute miles to O'Neill's driveway. I stayed outside with the pony and trap, while the others went in. An hour later, Philly came out with his arm in splints, the dark greatcoat over his shoulders, a white bandage from arm to neck; he had the solemn air of an archbishop. He neither spoke nor lifted his head on the way home.

Having unyoked the pony, I handed Kate the reins to take the animal to the stable. I got the hurricane lamp, lit it and went out to the haggard to push the trap back under the linnie. The curved lance-wood shafts felt smooth, springy and delicate, and to think of the weight they'd carried: their long slenderness disguised their strength. Hadn't expected to meet anybody else there again that night. A surprise then to see Kate coming over, as I was about to turn out the lamp. I'd take my leave of her so, and go home. She was the first to speak.

183

Thanks for driving us.

Think nothing of it.

I do appreciate what you did. Kate stood looking into my face, her manner so different from the way she'd been on the journey. What was this all about? She wasn't the type to blow hot one minute and cold the next. She couldn't have found out what'd happened to her precious brother, or else she wouldn't be so friendly. And that wasn't all.

Listen, can we talk? says Kate.

Isn't that what we're doing?

You know what I mean.

No, I don't know what you mean. She was being a bit presumptuous; I'd have to keep a certain remove, after all that coolness.

You do know what I mean, Kate insisted. Look, let's go someplace for a bit of privacy; I'd just like to talk to you.

What is there that can't be said here? I asked, turning round to face the hayshed.

Reluctant as I was to give in, it still felt good that Kate had approached me and wanted my attention; that this was sudden and unexpected made it all the more pleasing. So we moseyed over to the hayshed, checked that nobody was watching and went into the great opening in the middle that divided the shed in two, the hay from the straw. A ladder leaned against a shelf of hay that was only half the height of the rest of the bay. Kate climbed the ladder first. I held my foot on the bottom rung till she moved onto the shelf, and I followed. Mightn't turn out a bad old night after all.

I propped my back against a side wall that had been cut down, almost vertically, with a hay-knife. A night breeze must've risen: the hurricane lamp, still lighting, swung from its hook outside the linnie. Not that we could see it from our perch, but the line of shadow, thrown slantwise against the wall of straw across from us, was swaying. The movement had an eerie feel to it; as though the shadow possessed life: an essence absorbed from the object that caused it. Back and forth, in time to the beat of a heart. And there was more here than mere shadow.

Looking up, you could just make out the lattice-work shapes to one of the steel frames that supported the roof. The visible bit suggested the rest of the structure which was invisible and that you knew was there, hidden: a series of stringers, struts and stays to make up the entire carcass. For a moment, it seemed to heave in and out, like a ribcage breathing; a living thing, and we were under it, on the inside. Its eyes were there someplace among the shadows watching us. I didn't like being watched, studied, in this dismal light; would've preferred the pitch black of pure night, outside beyond, where there were no shadows to hide prying eyes. The thought that I might be a little manic in myself only added to the phobia coming on. A boy's phobia maybe, but it couldn't be helped. I was so obsessed by it, I scarcely noticed Kate turn and put her arms around my neck. She was in a different world from me.

Look, Will, I'm sorry for being distant with you, says she.

Was that what she called it: the previous two years' stand-off between us? Distant, how are you! And here she was all fervent and cloying, like it'd been a thing or nothing. She even expected a warm response; like I ought to jump for bloody joy to be the object of her affections again. Some neck! It was hard to resist her body near me, though; the shape of her face, barely outlined in this miserable light, and the prospect of comfort for most of an hour. Another little tug of her arms about my neck, an extra, ardent squeeze by way of evoking a response, as if that was all was needed to erase memories.

The shadows kept moving, sometimes jerkily, but mainly in slow, even strokes. Then, a shape I hadn't noticed before: a dark object swayed with the other shadows. A cold shiver ran up my spine. A spectre for all the world like a human body dangling from a rope. The night was fucked. I had to get away.

What's wrong? says Kate, when I brought my hands up and removed her arms from my neck.

Look, I thought you just wanted to talk, says I. I'm not ready for all this – which wasn't true, but I could hardly tell her I was afraid of shadows. A lot has happened since we were last together, says I. There's you and your copper man?

You put paid to him, well and good, says she.

What do you mean? I asked. But she only laughed.

He must've dropped you like a hot cake, and that's why you're so friendly now with me, says I. That remark, surely, would set her back on her heels.

But it didn't. Look, he meant nothing to me, says she. Her hands found mine, and she squeezed my fingers. To be so openly accessible, with this turn-about of manner, made her vulnerable; like a beggar exposed to the whims of the one who answers his door-knock. Some effort it must've taken her — knowing the person she was, and her pride. A response greater than what I could muster was called for.

But I couldn't avail myself of the opportunity, or rise to the occasion. Wished I could've: it might be a different world today. My agitation was too demanding to be appeased by words or finger-squeezing affection; I also resented her overbearing manner. To insult her was all I could manage.

Did the copper man give you a good whack of his baton when yous were up here on the hay? says I. And I pushed her hands away. She stepped back from me, and I went down the ladder.

The spectre turned out to be a bundle of old jute sacks that'd been tidied up out of the way, suspended by a long rope from a girder above in the roof. It was as still as the other immovable objects round there, yet its shadow moved the way the other shadows moved. Were shadows more alive than the objects that caused them? I went closer, to satisfy my curiosity. A queer thing though: the bundle wasn't moving back and forth, left or right, but slowly turned in a circle, like an eddy spiralling in on itself. Somebody must've passed by and spun it round. It would remind you of the river with its turnholes, where both the lightest and the weightiest of things are drawn inwards to the centre, before being pulled under.

I just had to step back, and get away; I even ran.

SIXTEEN

Simon

Take a couple of days to think about it, Nora, I said.

She folded the letter from Kate Kelly, put it in the envelope and handed it back to me. I don't need to think about, she said. But maybe you do. So, you take the time to ponder on it, see what you want to do and then we can talk. In the meantime, why not write and ask that lady what her conditions are. There's always snags; nothing's ever for free.

I decided to drop a line to my mum as well, to find out if she'd heard anything about this, and how she might feel about it. After all, the arrival of her son and his family back on her doorstep would cause a stir around there, talk that she mightn't like. Never one for drawing attention to herself, she could do without the side-looks and the begrudgery from a few of her neighbours. *Why should her son be given that farm? What right has he to come here from England? Land grabbers!* That sort of thing. My mum would run a mile if she heard it.

Apart altogether from the effect on herself, she'd want only the best for me and my family. And if I remember rightly, she was pleased – sad but pleased, at the time; you know what I mean – to see me emigrate. You'll have an opportunity to better yourself, she said. There's no hope you'll ever make anything of yourself in these parts, no chance. You're right to get away.

For that reason, my mum might not want to see me back there. Not that her opinion would impinge on me, one way or the other, once my mind was made up, but at the same time I'd like to know how she'd feel about it. On the other hand, she might be over the moon to have her son and a young family running round her heels, paying her the attention she never got. So I'd like to hear back from my mum as soon as possible; told her so, too.

It would do little Bob a power of good to get to know his gran. I think he's a bit like her: the same eyes, anyway. The open space would be good for him. And close to nature, he'd get to experience the essential things: the grain being sowed and shoots coming up in springtime, and the crops getting harvested in the autumn. If he were to take to the farming, he might even have a future ahead of him. And he'd have enough room to park his bike.

I don't know about May, though. She'd have her

own bedroom, but that's about it. Might be too late for her now to adapt to the country life. She's already a little city miss, I'm thinking, with her dolls and nice things, and would not take kindly to the smells or cope with the muck that goes with living in a farmyard. Such a change mightn't be the best for her schooling, either. There's an awful lot of pros and cons to be taken into account.

As far as Nora's concerned, I doubt she'd have difficulty adapting to the change. She already knows what farming life is like: having been raised on a small-holding back in Galway. Still talks about the chores she had to do: going to the well for water, milking cows and feeding the animals. So it's not like I'd be dragging some dolly bird in high heels along. That alone might be the deciding factor yet.

Mustn't forget, either, Nora still has to give me her opinion; I'd like to know what that'll be. Didn't take her long to make up her mind, did it? She's like that. Though she probably still wonders about the snags and conditions of it all, and will clock up the possible debits and credits like it were a balance sheet.

Anyway, Miss Kelly has now got the electricity installed, so it wouldn't take a lot to upgrade the house. And my wife ought to have a better lifestyle than what she was used to, back in Galway.

* * *

As Nora suggested, I wrote to Kate Kelly to ask why she wanted to hand her property over to me, and what it was she was looking for in return – what was the catch? Supposing my wife and her didn't get along: two women in the one kitchen and all that? It happens.

Miss Kelly replied, apologizing for not having made things clearer before. Her intention, she said, was to carry on pottering about the yard and looking after the cows, while I'd farm the land and manage the other livestock. The sale of stock and produce would be my doing, likewise all the sales and handling of the income. She'd always keep her room and draw a wage. She'd take an active interest in things for a while, by way of advice, to get me back into farming. All her intentions were above board, no hidden conditions. If in the event of some unsolvable difference between us, or that my wife and her couldn't exist under the one roof, my family and I'd leave, and things would revert to the way they were before. On my arrival, we would go to a solicitor and have an agreement drawn up. She had already talked to my mother about this. And my mother had told her she'd write to me. As regards differences, says she, there wouldn't ever be a problem that two willing people couldn't overcome.

The reason for her offer seemed clear: loneliness – or madness. I began to get the picture. She was sad on account of the farm; the place needed somebody to work it, a person she could depend on to eventually take over, and she needed an interest. I felt sorry for her, but what had all of it got to do with me? Why would I uproot my family to facilitate the notions of some old dear? It was risky; mightn't work out, and then we'd have to hit the road again.

The one thing that's been in the back of my mind since the lady made me this offer: how come I'm the one she wants to hand over her farm to? I just ain't got a satisfactory answer to that yet.

My mum, in her letter, enquired about May, Bob and Nora, and how they were doing. She talked about the makes of cars that the neighbours had – never could understand this obsession she has with motors – and what the weather was like over there. That's how most of her letter was taken up. Only near the end did she mention that she'd been talking to Kate Kelly.

Son, says she, you do what you want; I won't influence you, one way or the other. And isn't it very good of Miss Kelly to make you this offer? Of course, I'd be delighted to see you back home. But why did you go away in the first place, if not to escape the very drudgery you'd be returning to? While things are improving, there's still a long way to go. And the narrow-mindedness of some people here hasn't changed one iota, either.

My mum is reacting exactly as expected.

However, and like she said, I'm going to do what I want. But what's best for all of us will be taken into consideration.

As Nora reads the letters, and we get down to talk about it, there's a sort of glint in her eye.

SEVENTEEN

His injury marked the start of Philly Kelly going into himself. For a fellow on the go non-stop, it couldn't have been easy for him to come to a standstill. Such an instant standstill! Had to be a shock to the system. Those long legs and gifted fingers, that'd rested only while he slept, must've become confused, frustrated to be so bone idle. Nothing he could do, though, but grin and bear it.

Having to put up with things is what's set aside only for the everyday person, your ordinary run-of-the-mill fogey here; not meant by Mother Nature to be the lot of great worthies. Game birds, pure-bred horses and persons with the luck of cut cats walk the high roads of this world, where history is made and at least one great deed a day is a must from each gallant. While here on the low road, your ordinary wayfarer has to trundle on, put up with things and do the long penances. Our allotment. That's not to say the blessed ones on the high ground don't suffer, but their pain is different: has special meaning, significant, especially when fatally dramatic. And gets marked down in history. To the high-roader, suffering is the exception not the rule, and when it comes, it never drags out the way it does with lesser mortals.

It must have been torture for Philly to be so cruelly knocked from his perch, and then have to put up with being idle. Sad to see him so pathetic-looking. Did I have sympathy for him? Sympathy! A certain pity, maybe, but hardly sympathy. The hurling was the first to go. He missed all the championship matches during the '26 season, which ran into the following year. That great team broke new ground by reaching the District Final, played in February 1927.

In the gold and olive-green of old, Philly too should've strutted out onto that Bellefield pitch, and felt the vibrations of excitement coming in waves from the crowd. He'd not only have had the honour of winning, but the chance to show off his finely honed skills to the greatest number of admirers. No doubt they'd have roared their appreciation when he caught a ball and danced a side-step to go on a solo run a good thirty yards upfield. He'd have gracefully swung his stick, the one I had crafted to be a wand of creation rather than the weapon of destruction, and thumped the lump of hemp-stitched leather a full sixty yards, over the crossbar for another point; to send his team onwards to an even greater victory than the one they did actually eke out that Sunday. And even more important: how much greater the stories would've been, had he played on the day.

What we'd have had to listen to! Not that Philly's scores might've added much to the final tally – after all, the team did win – but imagine the extra richness and colour to stories down the years. To this day, thirty-three years on, old lads on high stools and elbows to the bar above in Murphy's sip and remember that game in silence. Each can tell you exactly where he stood on the bank along the sideline, the view he had of the particular piece of action he's dreaming of and, indeed, the very spot he'd left his bike before going in.

Kenny's for bikes, Kenny's for pikes is still Jim Rowe's catchphrase. There hanging out of his nightly pint above in Murphy's, he'd surely remember Philly's skills from that day. Being a man for leaving the darker things of the past behind him, Rowe would've forgotten the night he put the revolver to Philly's ear and threatened to blow his head off. Long gone, anyway, are the days of trenchcoats, slouch hats and Smith and Wessons – probably rusted out by now. But Rowe, who still holds sway in any company, counts the stories of Philly's hurling prowess on a level with his own adventures. He never talks about the insurgent stuff; leaves it to doughtier boys, the *gaiscí* who in the Trouble Times wouldn't go outside at night for a leak. It didn't stop them, though, from blowing their trumpet or collecting their old IRA pensions. The same fuckers that keep that pot stirred round here still.

It's not often nowadays you'll see Ben Rowe, Jim's funny brother, inside in Murphy's. He seldom stirs beyond his front gate, and the fun is long gone out of him too. But on the odd occasion he makes it there for a pint, somebody always calls on him to sing the ballad about the hurlers, in which the name of each player is mentioned. Had Philly been on that team, he'd have had a full line of verse all to himself.

The music had to go too. Play an instrument with only one hand! Must've had an even worse effect on Philly than forfeiting the hurling. Kellys' kitchen lost its sparkle, and people eased off calling; probably they didn't want to be an imposition on Philly – or maybe it was because they were fickle hoors. Anyway, they stayed away. And the dancing stopped.

Nothing in Kellys' but dour pusses and long faces. Pat the hat in one chimney corner, and the old doxy forever by the fanners, guessing the weather. There's rain on the way, she'd say; I can feel it in my bones. Too busy asking questions to be questioned, her eyes ready to ward off looks in her direction, like she had secrets, or hurts, to protect. As if anyone could be bothered to ask her anything. If hurling was even mentioned, she'd cut the socks off Philly – obviously she hadn't found out what'd happened to his arm; fair play to him, after all. When she lost her temper, she'd give the wheel of the fanners a twirl to send a cloud of ash and crackly *gríosóga* up the chimney. Who'd want to see that?

At the time, I was glorying too much in Philly's misfortune to think about his state of mind, or guess that events might take a turn for the worse. This down I'd always had on him could at last be savoured. He'd got his comeuppance, and I'd no longer – at least for the time being – have to take a back seat to the shagger, but I felt no compunction whatsoever for my handiwork. Why should I? Mind, I did call to see him: to be supportive, *moryah*, even sympathetic – as far as I could like, without being too barefaced. Things had gone full circle; all the more reason to enjoy my revenge. That sweet luscious thing, the way Maysie Dunne had been luscious a long time before, and like any savoury, it had to be taken slowly, in small portions, to allow its flavours to tickle the palate. And as with all the best of occasions, it ought to be enjoyed quietly, no fuss.

Isn't it very nice of you now, Will, to call and see how Philly's doing? says Nanny Kelly, rasping it out. She didn't mean a word of it, but, no matter, what she said washed off me. I was immune to her at last.

Might've even given her a lash back; you're looking pale, missus, you're not sick or anything, are you? A subtle dig, food for thought while she twirled her fecking fanners, and imagined she still held her looks like a young one. But I said nothing; my being there alone seemed enough to unsettle her. Anyway, trump cards are best held close.

That my presence would unsettle Philly, or help to unhinge his state of mind, didn't strike me. Just wanted to grig him; to indulge myself a little. I passed no all-out blatant remarks to raise his hackles, and only ever faintly hinted at our row. Occasionally, I'd call there in the evening, before Kate got home – better to give her a miss for a while. Philly was bound to be either sitting in the house, with a glum face, or outside fiddling with some chore, like attempting – with one hand! – to chop sticks with a billhook. Only he'd get agitated and then walk off in frustration. Oh, that was sweet to watch. You should rest up, you know, Philly, I'd say. You'll heal all the quicker.

It was getting to him that he couldn't work the land. Instead, his father was back following the pair of horses – that year, the Mullán, their highest field, had to be ploughed. Pat Kelly had long before given over all the skilled work to his son. Philly was really the farmer, while his father pottered about doing odd jobs. But Pat the hat, the odd-job man, was back in harness. Must've distressed Philly even more.

Are you sure you don't want to be driven anywhere? says I, out of pity. Half hoped he wouldn't take up the offer; didn't fancy having to yoke the pony and trap just to amuse him after my day's work. Hoped he'd refuse, too, when I suggested going to look at ash trees, that some of them were ready to cut. Hurleys, under the circumstances! Hadn't thought of the good of it till I'd said it. Of course, he refused. Refused everything, he did; wanted to do nothing.

Philly had an upturn of mood shortly before the District Final, or so I thought. The last few times I'd called on him, well into the month of February '27, he seemed more talkative. Let's take a look at those trees you mentioned, says he. A gesture of friendship at last?

We walked the path me and Kate used to saunter along. At one point he turned and stared at me, an unsettling moment. I've not forgotten that gaze, after all the years. His eyes were back in his head, the whites gone yellow, framed within dark circles and red rims, and for a second there I got a glimpse of an infernal torment. Some awful cursed anguish that's frightening even yet. He started to talk.

The first time since the row, he mentioned her name. That snowy-breasted pearl, whom the trouble had been all about, had come between our friend-ship since childhood. Maysie Dunne. That tumbling beauty of bygone days, who could still attract with the flash of a sultry eye: her name was up again to cause more trouble. And I'd thought that our little dalliance – fling, whatever – no longer bothered Philly, or wasn't worth making a fuss over. But how wrong can you be? It did bother him, on top of all the other bother he had, and it showed; part of the anguish in his eyes. He was far too vulnerable a specimen for such thorns in his side, like a thoroughbred – the lesser breeds for the rough terrain. I wished I could apologize or do something, but I was stuck for words.

Because Philly was besotted, he went on about Maysie, what she meant to him: more than all his family put together. That if she were to leave him he couldn't take it. A total bloody obsession! But his intensity was immense, if not frightening. And in matters of the heart, he could never be anything but an open book. Damn him to hell! That trait, too, only made him more likeable.

What else could I say in the circumstances? Is everything all right between the two of you? Are yous back together?

Yeah, I've met her once or twice, says he. But it's not the same, never will be: I look at her differently now. There was no blame in his voice; he was only telling it as it was, like a newsreader on the wireless.

He was, however, seeing Maysie Dunne again: a hard fact, and something, if not progress. I said that I hoped things would improve between them. Wished them well.

But hold on! What was happening here? Philly had become so palsy-walsy, and trusting of me, all of a sudden. While I might've won back some of his confidence, was it not peculiar why he'd tell me such personal stuff? A plan to get my sympathy? So that I'd leave his doll alone, not go after her or try to wipe his eye. So that was it. And to think I'd imagined him an open book. Wasn't I some *leibide*, too, to get taken in like that, for going soft on him – only a momentary lapse, though, on my part. Just a temporary slip.

An evening or two later, I bumped into Maysie in the village. I'd just come out of the post office. Hello, Maysie, how are you since the last time I saw you? *Last time I saw you* was said slowly to remind her, as if she needed reminding, of that evening of harmless fun we'd had; we hadn't met since. She was shivering in her fawn gabardine costume; no coat – hardly suitable attire for February.

Ah, I'm not too bad, says she.

How's things with Philly?

How do you think they are? says she, with a hang-dog look. A good enough answer. She was blue from the cold – blue from more than cold, what! I took off my army coat, the one I'd picked up second-hand at the fair of Borris in the fall of the year previous – which I wear yet – and placed it round her shoulders.

Come on, I'll walk you home, I says. You can tell me about it on the way. Her house was a short journey from the shop, so the walk was no big deal. Have you clapped eyes on him lately?

Met him once or twice, says she.

Why did you have to go and tell him about us? What were you thinking?

I just said you and I had met. I mentioned nothing else.

What did you want to tell him anything for? Surely you'd've known that when you give away one thing, he'd suspect more. Philly is not an eejit. What the hell was wrong with you, Maysie?

It was all your fault, says she. If you hadn't tricked me into going with you up the banks, none of this would've happened.

If you hadn't opened your big mouth, says I, he'd never have found out.

She flashed the brown eyes, took the coat from her shoulders, threw it at me and then walked off. I turned to walk away but thought better of it. Maybe something could be salvaged, if I played the game right. So I trotted after Maysie and put my coat back over her shoulders. Her *taom* had eased. Nothing like a good frosty night for cooling the pot, old

Marty Nolan used to say. She might've cooled off, but you could tell she was still upset. Well, when Maysie was upset, there was no better man to console her. Though she'd probably tell Philly again.

That queer ritual of laying the flagstone over the horse's head in the middle of Kellys' floor had taken most of the day. The job was just done, when Kate came in from work. Philly started to lilt, and got her to dance on the new floor for a test. I listened to the sound off the flagstone while watching Kate's ankles and high-flying legs. I avoided her eyes at all costs. Philly joined in the dance, but moved only very gently because of his arm. That'll do, says he – the floor was ready; the stone had passed its test.

The whole operation had been more of a ritual than a job of work, a sacred rite of some kind. And like church rituals, I didn't understand this strange caper either. I'd carried out Philly's instructions to the letter: selecting the flag in the quarry, knocking the head off Doran's cob, removing the flesh and laying the floor. It was like I had assisted in a pagan rite, an acolyte in attendance to the celebrant. Philly was the arch-priest. All we lacked was the garb. The chief celebrant had remained solemn through it all, distant.

Anyway, the dance would go on. Win, lose or draw, the team's achievements would be celebrated. Philly's contribution, since it couldn't be on the hurling pitch, would be to throw a hooley. And he was looking forward to the night; his spirit was up. Or so I thought.

The light had gone and the place was in full swing when I got there. I had heard the music while coming up the road: a giddy bloody whirl of a sound drawing all things unto itself. The pipe-chanter twittered like a pair of larks one minute, cried like a starving baby the next, lording it over the fiddle, flute and box; only one box being played that night. Outside, men in circling groups chattered against the music; inside, they'd've had to speak into each other's ears: much easier to talk outside, despite the chilly air. And on that occasion, talk would take priority over music and dance. For everybody had their own special memories of the previous Sunday: where they'd stood, where they'd left bikes, and the banter with supporters of the other team. They especially wanted to swap moments from the game. This was a night to indulge in story. Not quite what Philly'd had in mind.

He listened to two of the team's forwards inside the porch tell each other about scores they'd got. For once, their episodes would leave him out. And not being part of the shared limelight, he was on the fringe, hardly noticeable. He was definitely excluded. He went into the kitchen. The music lacked the vigour that the stories had. The resonance off the floor during a dance, though marvellous, failed to captivate people; they were fascinated by other things. Philly's efforts seemed to've been wasted. He'd mistimed the night; misjudged its expectations. From one group to the next he drifted, from one person to another. But all he could contribute was to listen, while dazzling butterflies flitted and flashed their wares through stories told. For once he was the moth at the glass.

No sign of Maysie Dunne either. She'd have been a crutch for him. I went to the kitchen window to see was she inside. The place was teeming with hurlers' bright red faces, luxuriating in the glory of Sunday, and two couples half-heartedly click-clacked a half-set. Still no sign of Maysie. Why hadn't she turned up on the night? I remained outside, near the window. Philly was bent over the dresser with a pencil in his hand, writing on a notepad. He tore out the sheet, put it in his pocket and turned round. Those eyes, back in his head like an old man's, spotted me: that inferno was in them again.

Later, he came outside, sort of wandered out. Nobody heeded or turned to talk to him. He edged his way past fellows as if he were alone, past me by the window, without acknowledging me, and out to the haggard. Curiosity made me follow at a distance. The lantern was hanging from the beam of the linnie it had hung from when Kate and I had last talked. Philly took it down, lit it and crooked it back up. A haggard full of swaying shadows, as if he'd wanted it that way. He turned round to look at everything in the place, or what could be taken in from the limited light, like a lad at a train station who'd turn one last time to his family and search out friends' faces for goodbye glances. Except there was nobody in the place, no one but the old friend he couldn't see. A din came from the yard inside. Still looking back, he walked slowly towards the hayshed. He paused before going into the opening between the hay and the straw, into the dark, among the swaying shadows; where sorcery was at its strongest.

How was I to know, there and then, that the night was cursed, and that its effects, too, were numbing me. To this very day, I keep asking if the spell could've been broken and Philly prevented from doing what he was about to do next. Could I have stopped him? Indeed, I did suspect what he was up to, without fully believing it – allowing that my imagination was running away with itself.

Oh, but it was no imaginary thing; I knew all right. Could make out his shape – the way it went about things – what he was up to. Maybe even something inside me urged him on, to step out into the black void. Numbed by anticipation, among the shadows of the haggard, I stood and watched. And wondered.

What did go on in that brain of his? Some little cog must've seized up momentarily to drive him to this? Was it the ritual of laying the flagstone over the horse's head that spellbound him? Shouldn't have been allowed in the first place, or the dance let go ahead. Somewhere along the line, this sorcery ought to have ended, been ended. It had, probably, all become too much for him, and driven him to walk in there, alone. Something drove him. And forced him to lower, then untie, the bundle of sacks. To bring the rope with him up the ladder – the same ladder Kate and I had gone up, and in the one spot – to noose the rope and place it like a scarf about his neck. And all the while I watched.

Then his last act. The weekly newspaper, the following Saturday, reporting the inquest, said that after fixing the rope he had kicked the ladder from under him. A jerked swing. The jiggle would change to a circling movement. Another motion also: his body would spiral round itself because of the coiled make-up of the hemp rope, like someone had passed by and spun it. An eddy spiralling in on itself, the turnhole of the river where both the lightest and the weightiest of things are pulled to its centre and then under, would take him. All would go still and black. Black within black. Nothing stirred much, but the rope slowing down, the din and the faded music from the yard. All slowed to suit the sway of the lantern and shadows.

EIGHTEEN

The place was haunted by demon crows as I came up the road for Philly's wake. Off the tops of bare beeches at the lower side of Kellys' yard, their black sharp shapes came and went. Those shrill banshees of the high branches pecked each other, fluttered and screeched like all hell had broken loose. Having spent the day scanning the countryside, here they were again home to roost; in another few weeks, those treetops would be blemished with dark nests. As with all creatures of the seasons, they too had their rush of blood, chores to be got on with. And their miserable, pitiless hearts dictated that they complain impatiently about the change of weather slowing down the progress of spring.

Kellys' pony and trap, along with four others on the road, was tied at the upper side of the yard entrance, ready. At a time like this you'd notice the familiar things, even search them out. I stopped across the road to count the iron uprights in the lower section of the half-gate. There were twenty, as well as the centrepiece that went right to the top before dividing into two spirals. At his leisure, old Pat had painted that gate with red lead the previous summer. I stood picturing his black frame stoop and rise slowly. Would he ever paint it again?

Another step forward would give me a view of the yard and the door. The last time I'd been at that spot, the sound of a pipe-chanter could be heard over the fiddle, flute and box; only one box being played that night. The music was still going on in my head. I half expected to see the same men standing round in circling groups chattering, swapping moments from the previous Sunday week's hurling match. Could almost hear their words, and feel the pride, brought to our place, which promised so much. But I tried to put the music and faces from my head; it wasn't proper to think such things at this time.

Then came a full view of the yard. Many of the same men were again standing outside the door. This time they were dressed in black, silent and bunched together against the biting breeze. There were strangers among them: probably Kellys' relations out from town.

I froze. For also in the yard, a man in a tailcoat and tall hat stood at the head of a pair of horses, hand to the winkers. One plume, the colour of the men's suits, rose from each of the horses' heads and fanned out like it was part of the dark clouds overhead. Animals and minder stood motionless before the hearse, ready. The time was getting near: less than an hour before the removal.

A few feet away, a dozen or so Rhode Island Reds pecked across the yard, regardless. Bits of oaten straw and chaff tumbled over each other in the breeze up the yard; then twirled round like an eddy, or a *shee gwee*.

Inside, the parlour door was open. Men and women in their best black sat, chatted and laughed like they'd not seen each other for years, or as if all their cousins were home from America. Kellys' china was laid out on the parlour table; sandwich portions, slices of cake, buns and an assortment of biscuits – but no pretzels – were on matching plates. Those same plates had seldom seen the light of day: they shone so much like glass. Unopened porter bottles sat in crates near the door.

I hesitated in the porch for a moment, thinking of other times, before turning the opposite way. The smell of baked bread met me going into the kitchen, but I didn't feel hungry.

The only person there that mattered sat beside her mother. And Nanny was in her old spot – the comfort of familiarity for her, too? – twirling the wheel of the fanners, out of habit. No need, for a fine fire already blazed on the hearth. Her head leaning against her daughter's shoulder, the old woman sobbed dry tears. Her ululations, though, were barely audible. What'll I do, what'll I do? she said over and over again. As if by its own accord, the fanners stirred and keened in time to the sound of the old woman.

Kate showed her lamentation only in her blue heavy eyes. She raised them to look at me, nodded slightly and turned her head away, inward towards her mother. Pat sat in his corner, unaware of, or indifferent to, my being there.

The others in the kitchen were mostly local women, whose big hearts glowed as did the reds of their faces, commandeering the run of the household chores to deal out the hospitality for the wake. Someone offered me tea. But I refused, stepped aside and climbed the stairs.

It was the first time I'd ever put my head up there, in the inner sanctum. I turned on the landing to face the far room, the only door that was open, and stopped for a moment to get myself together.

A banister under the handrail felt coarse; I put my hand to it again to check, and picked up a splinter. A gaping knot in the wood had been left unsanded. He must've known; he ought to've seen to it. How exact, though, he'd been about other things. Oh aye, take that day in the quarry, when nothing but the best would satisfy him. Well, Philly, look where all your outwardly perfection had got you, in the heel of the hunt?

213

The half-open door at the far end signified something. And why was he in the end room, the big one over the parlour? I'd thought that was where the old pair slept. That hardly mattered any more. Forty-nine polished flooring boards I counted, to the open door – half-open door. Whoever had put them in did a good job: not so much as a razor blade could you run between them.

I got a start. Three patches along the corridor partition lit up. The evening sun on its last legs had somehow managed to break through the clouds. No more, though, than a momentary thing.

In the chill of the room, I can't face him. And the light's poor, darker than the trout-brown of other times. A black wooden candlestick stands tall, stark at either side of the head of the bed. A blessed candle flickers in each. A sprig of palm – the only green thing there – lies across a glass bowl of holy water on a small table near him.

The double bed, with its brass posts, no doubt belongs to this room. The old pair's bed is now his. Probably where Philly was born. The first place and the last, the start and finish of a thing: the beginning and end all at once together. A final ritual of hidden meanings from some nether world: the sort of send-off he'd've wanted. Loved old rites and symbols, he did.

Eight people there in the room – off counting again. A few ancient women, dark shawls over their heads eerily like the baleful crows outside, perch on chairs along two sides. Well used to death, this is maybe a little more than their usual spectacle, as the balls of their beady eyes hop. In days gone by, these women would've been keening and wailing the roof off our heads. The rest of the people, elbows on chairs, kneel.

That racket from the parlour underneath grows loud; breaks in on our quiet. One old woman starts the rosary – that'll put manners on them. The chant of prayer rises and drowns out the noise. All of a sudden, the voices from below stop. Glad of the distraction, I kneel at the nearest empty chair, and drone along with the prayers. But my heart and mind aren't in it.

The roller blinds are down three-quarter ways on the two windows, keeping out whatever evening light that's left, and block the view. But I don't need to look: I've got a picture of what's out there.

All of Springmount lies beyond. A vast place in so many ways. Springmount in the springtime. Did he ever think of that? The name for a ballad, maybe, or one of those hornpipes he made up in praise of life. Philly celebrating life!

Across the fields, up the commons and over the mountain itself, a change of guard is about to take place at this hour. Dandelions and daisies close their petals, cowslips bow their heads; daytime creatures and all things dependent on the sun get ready to kneel down at the onset of dark. For soon, it'll be the turn of the night-watch: the beings that come from the bowels of the earth to rise, patrol and hunt the land. Watch out for glowing eyes and shadows prowling behind trees. Wicked night scavengers that prey on the remains of pure-bred beings.

Here in the room, the litany drones on: *Pray for us, pray for us. Keep us from all harm. Pray for us.* It's safe, though, in here in this room; nothing but the dead can touch the dead.

Footsteps come up the stairs and onto the landing beyond; more than one pair. Wish they'd stay away and not intrude on this righteous silence. There's the sound of a person shuffling along the landing. Then the door opens wider. Kate comes through, with an arm round her mother's shoulder.

Shock at the sight of him again seizes Nanny, makes her go rigid and prevents sobbing. Pat follows, but I can't read his expression; he looks odd without the hat. The prayers stop. Haven't seen his face yet; time is running on.

The bed holds a human shape. Arms over the sheets and hands joined, a string of beads sits round his thumbs and between his fingers. I try to count the fingers, but they're too white. His face is less white, more waxen, like my mother's. His nose is too prominent, and nostrils too cavernous. Eyes are barely closed. No expression of the mouth.

I try to check his neck, but the shirt-collar is right up to the chin. The back of his head rests so lightly on the pillow, he could be asleep. Having a nap after his day's work, fresh shirt on before going out for the night to meet Maysie.

Gone? Philly couldn't be gone. He's part of the place. He'll never leave. Can't say goodbye to him.

The newspaper report would say that, under sad circumstances, a man had died at his home. That the deceased was a young man of good character and friendly disposition, and the rash act by which he'd met his death came as a shock to the people of the district. That his father found him the next morning. And a brief note pencilled on ordinary notepaper, discovered on his person, was produced at the inquest. That the coroner said the note was only of importance as indicating the state of mind of the deceased.

Outside in the yard, a crowd had gathered. The empty coffin still lay in the hearse, and there were more prayers to be said up in the room: a while yet to wait. Not wanting to talk, I went out to the haggard to be on my own.

Abruptly, the presence of the shed, which I'd somehow managed to put out of mind, loomed before me. Light of day not quite gone, I could make out the black hole below between the hay and straw. Empty.

Then a movement; something stirred. Surely no person would venture there this evening. There it was again. I went down by the side of the haggard, quietly over to the opening and peered round the corner. She was a little way back, almost underneath where he would've been, sitting on a bundle of straw.

It was hard to know what to say to Maysie. And I didn't want to talk. Went over, sat beside her and put my arm round her shoulder.

Don't, says she, he's watching us. She'd misread my intentions. I could hardly blame her for that. From the hoarseness of her voice, she'd been shouting.

I didn't take my arm away, though; sort of guessed she didn't want me to. Could've asked what she was doing there, but what was the point, when the reply wouldn't matter. Wouldn't change what'd happened.

I'm going to have a baby, says she.

I couldn't ask. It wasn't my place to ask. Besides, no answer would alter her state, or the facts behind it. And it had to be true: the girl didn't know how to lie. So I said nothing.

We sat there silently, side by side, till we heard a stirring. The sound from the yard of hooves clomping over stones. Time to go. We saw the hearse pull out through Kellys' gateway. And me and Maysie joined the group walking directly behind. Out and down the road.

I'd never witnessed such a large funeral. We'd turned the first bend in the road, while, behind us, the light of the leading pony and trap still hadn't moved off. Our only light came from the carbide lamps on either side of the hearse.

Is he going to get a proper burial? she asks. Was that all was bothering her?

Of course he is, I said. It's not like that any more.

Rumour had it, Philly wasn't supposed to get a church burial, or be laid to rest within hallowed ground. It was all a rumour, though. The only person I'd ever heard of to be denied the full rites was an old Fenian from town, some time in the last century. Whether Philly would get a High Mass or not, only the next morning would tell. But for this night, he'd lie inside the church above. For definite, Philly was gone from us.

While Maysie was left to take care of herself – and not just herself. She needed minding. She was owed that much; and so was Philly.

Over the bridge, past the end of our lane and up the road to the village, Maysie walked all the way beside me in near silence. I was her only comfort along the trail behind Philly's remains. She kept step with me, and I accepted how it was.

And that's the way the thing went on.

NINETEEN

Simon

I wish they'd shut up. The passengers' chatter is like a Saturday-night rant down the pub coming up to closing. The racket has increased noticeably over the last while. Excitement, no doubt, but something else is mixed in – tiredness, I suppose. This journey is such a drag: six hours on the train from Paddington and a three-hour trip then on this old tub, the *St Andrew*, out of Fishguard. Roll on Rosslare. We must be nearly there.

It wouldn't be so bad without the kids along. They keep asking if we're there yet. No, not even 'alfways, I say.

Are we 'alfways yet?

Just about, I say, trying to sound as dreary as them.

Ah, no! Fed up, they settle back to an uneasy sleep. You'd tell them anything to quell expectations. May is wrapped in a tartan rug the landlady gave her for the journey, and rests her head against my wife's leg. Himself, in his fawn wool coat, is stretched out here on my side along the seating, the same as his sister. With any luck, they won't tune in to the latest stir on board.

We're nearly in now, says the fat woman in a red coat. I noticed her earlier; she has herself plonked over by a window, and kept lookout for the entire trip. What she sees is anyone's guess. Any time me and jockser here went to look, all we could see was black night, with only the hint of a line between sky and sea.

If I were near that old blabbermouth right now, I'd clobber her. Nora, too, leans over and whispers to me: Hope they didn't hear that. She tries to muffle May's ears by tucking folds of the rug like a scarf round her head. But you never can tell with young ones, whether they're asleep or not. The old narwhal in red by the window stands up to get a better view. Must think she's the blooming navigator. When she repeats herself louder than before, Nora winces and tries to improve on her muffling skills. But too darn late: May's head pops up. Jockser here, too, stirs to life, rubs his eyes and looks up at me. He has to satisfy himself as to what's happening and heads for the nearest vacant window pane. I drag myself after him.

A line of lights along the pier brightens the water

221

beyond the ship, and the port gradually comes into focus. The long pier like a human arm, complete with elbow, reaches out to pluck us from the night. I'm beginning to have second thoughts about coming back: signs of the claustrophobia I used to have before I left. At least they've got electricity nowadays. Lady Kate's even got it on the farm: said so in one of her letters. Should've asked her if she's got running water in the house yet. Best to look on the bright side. Still can't help feeling unsure.

Down the gangway and onto the wharf. What? Could put dingy music to this: ports and railway stations, coming and going. Talk about changes! Don't see that conditions have improved much in the fifteen years odd since I last came through here. They're using the same old cranes on the cargo, and still sling cars from the hold. Shouldn't they have one of those openings in the side for driving on and off? And look, the train has still got a steam engine – I thought that even here they would've switched to diesel by now.

At least the train draws up alongside – it has to: little or no roadway to the shore. So over we trot, bag and baggage, and on we get. Just as well we sold our chattels before coming: would've been impossible to travel with the stuff we had. The old squeeze-box is now the bulkiest thing. Great. Here's a compartment all to ourselves – I know it's first class; well, let them shift us. We'll spread out what we have on the seats and nobody else will come in. Bloody hell, look who's stopping at our door! The sea-witch in the red coat, and she's coming in. Hey, you and me, Bob, we'll command the window seats this time. I've seen this dame in action on the boat . . . No, that's all right, missus, you come sit yourself down here; a sad day when we can't make room for a lady. Close that door properly, little Bob, and keep out the draught.

My name is Maggie Brophy; what's yours? says she. People that know me call me Mag the Mumps. That's because I had them real bad – the mumps, I mean, sorry. When I was little, I was very sick; nearly died they tell me. I don't remember. Do you remember when you were little? Oh, what am I talking about? Yous are young and little. I must be going crackers. This journey would drive anyone crackers, wouldn't it?

We slow down. Am I glad that the train journey wasn't long.

We're getting off here, Missus . . . Brophy.

Miss will do fine, thank you: never married, you see. Now don't get me wrong, I've had many a chance, plenty of offers. But men, you know what the men are like: say one thing and mean another; can't be trusted. The old dame has turned to address Nora.

A tunnel ahead, I say. We'll close the window. I remember it now, see. I try to work up a head of excitement to distract May and Bob from the old one's bias. We're nearly in, I shout, repeating her words from the boat. Let's get our backsides out before it moves off. No, that wouldn't do, missus. Come on, May, wake up, that's it. Of course it's a station. Not a very nice thing to say, young lady. Yes, we get off here, and we've got to find a cab – no, they don't call them that in these parts. Hackney men, I do believe.

Oh, this is my stop as well, says the old dame – must be about the age of my mum. I was back here only last Christmas. I'm from the town, you know. I've been over for more than thirty years. Are yous from the town?

No, we're not. Talk the leg off a pot, she would. Thirty years in England: you'd think she wasn't away a wet week. Come on, lads, let's go find the hackney man then. You take care of yourself now, missus, and we'll meet again some time . . .

As far as shocks and surprises go, I reckon it would take a whopper to show up on this old Richter scale. But see, I got this letter, out of the blue, that sent the hand right through the register. It had my name and address scrawled slantwise across a finger-daubed envelope. Inside, a sheet of blue notepaper had been scribbled on, up and down between black lines, like a drunken spider making a web. The name Chas Tobin was signed at the end. Big Cha Cha.

Kate Kelly asks you to come home, it said. She told me. A good idea? – a great idea. A few home truths might convince you. Since you're not who you no doubt think you are: the offspring of a certain Mr Will Byrne. By right, you too are a Kelly: the son of one Philip – known to his friends as Philly – Kelly. Your mother, Maysie Dunne, was Philly's girl until he died tragically. She was pregnant with you when the tragedy happened. Will Byrne then married your mother. He doesn't know it – he thinks you are his son – and I'd ask you to keep it that way. Your mother, your aunt Kate and myself have kept this quiet. I would not be telling you either but for needs must. It was agreed that I be the one to write and inform you.

The old doll and ourselves are the only passengers to get off here, and there's nothing on four wheels outside the station that even resembles a hackney. So I say to Nora and the kids to hang on, make themselves comfortable on the bench in the waiting room while I search the town and get some dopey git out of bed.

Outside, in the station yard, there's a blue Ford van that's seen better days; some old geezer sits behind the wheel. Pity the poor bugger; he's expecting someone, probably a son or daughter, off the boat-train and they haven't arrived. I'll ask him if he knows the name of a hackney across town. He's bald, got a big round face with two eyes like street-lights and this smile. I know that blooming face. The van door opens. 'Ello 'ello 'ello, cockney boy, says he, doing the accent. He begins to chuckle; it changes to a belly laugh. Big Cha's lost most of his hair since I saw him last.

'Ello, you baldy old bastard, I say. We shake hands, and I feel my own strength in the grip. Is this your contraption? I ask.

Of course it's mine! Whose do you think it is, the bishop's? Another fit of belly-laughing. He ain't changed that way. Blimey, it suddenly feels good to be back.

You mean to tell me you no longer walk across the Blackstairs?

I surely don't, and I don't drive this baby across them either.

Looks like it's been over many a mountain, I mutter, not thinking.

Hah?

Looks like it could be driven across any mountain: it's that sturdy. Fit for a bishop.

Ah, you never lost it, says he. Scrape off that accent, boy, and let the mountainy man out. She asked me to drive in and collect yous. Miss Kate. It's all right, no need to say nothing, she takes me into her confidence with things. Not many she'll trust, but I'm one of them. Your mam, Kate and myself go back a long way. So park yourselves here with me;

you're at my mercy for the remainder of the journey. Where's the rest of the clan? Go get them here quickly and we'll make a start for the hills. Oh, by the way, I hope you don't mind the tight squeeze in the van. Your father came along to meet you. He just went up the town to stretch his legs. You know how he is: can't bear to sit in the one spot for long.

Are yous from the mountains? asks the old dame – what's her name? Missus Mumps – Missus Brophy. She must have crept up unawares.

Why? asks Cha. He too is taken by surprise.

Because I once knew a boy from the mountains.

You knew him well? I ask her.

Know him well! Oh yes, you could say that. If I saw his face this minute, I'd recognize it, even after all the years. I never forget a face, you know, never.

He must've been good to you so, says Cha.

A very nice boy, and handsome. I often wonder what became of him.

Then I remember what she'd said on the train; that she was single. So I ask her: Is that why you never married? You never met the likes of this mountainy man since? I wink at Cha, who's still weighing her up.

You could say, she replies.

Blackstairs men for your life, says Cha and laughs. We have that effect on the women.

Are you sure, missus, it wasn't this old timer 'ere? I ask. Take a good look at him, he may have weathered a bit. I'm told he once had a way with the ladies.

No, it wasn't him, I tell you. My fellow was much better-looking nor that. The old dame then turns serious. And I never forget a face, she says. Cha's belly shakes.

What was his name? I ask. But she is already on her way.

I can see my old man walking over. Didn't realize that comings and goings at train stations was his cuppa tea. Maybe he's mellowed with age. Mind, he has aged: look at the stoop to his shoulders. Still 'n' all, it's good to see him. Now that I know he's not my real father, it frees up things between us, and I can look on him in a more favourable light. We might even get along. Hope he likes Nora; he'll surely take to the kids. He meets the old doll just under a streetlight and doffs his cap to her – there's a bit of a gent about him after all. Miss Mumps accepts his salute with a friendly *nice night*, and walks on. Yeah, it's good to be home.

TWENTY

That woman's face looks familiar. Or is it just a trick of the light from above? Could swear I know her from somewhere. But no matter.

Ah, he has arrived. He's over there now with the lug. Where's his family? Saw the train when I was across the town. As it rattled along the iron bridge over the river, found myself willing the thing on, wishing it well; as if it was alive and my good will towards it somehow made a difference. Felt fond of the long apparatus, its rows of lit windows, that carried a young family, the few people who strangely belonged to me. And the misgivings I'd had about coming to meet them disappeared. Glad now I came; relieved that they've landed. The shackles are gone too: no longer am I obliged to act out the father, now that Simon knows who he really is. Me and him might even catch up on things: hunt rabbits on the mountain, go to a match of a Sunday afternoon – and bring that young lad of his I see coming out of the station.

A lot of ice has melted recently. Myself and the clown, after all the years, now acknowledge each other's right to exist; almost like I'd never wanted to wring his neck. Thought he could read everybody's minds, he did, sticking his nose in things. It came about by necessity. One evening I went home, there was your man at the table like he owned the house. No surprise to see him: he'd always been a friend to herself, since Philly's time. But what had him there just then? Waiting for me, it seemed. I tried the cold quizzical face a farmer might give a trespasser who ignores the *Keep out* sign. And it didn't take him long to say what he'd come for. Kate Kelly wants to have a word with you, says he.

Does she, indeed. What does she want?

She'll let you know herself when she sees you, says he. A bit much, the tone of the summons.

Go and report back to your ladyship, says I. Tell her I'll call tomorrow evening. And I looked for signs on my wife's face: had she an inkling of what this was about? Oh, she knew all right, but there was nothing forthcoming.

It was the first time I'd been inside Kellys' door in over thirty years. Though I knew where everything was, I didn't know what to expect, or how I'd react to being in there again, meeting Kate face to face and talking to her. Her *come in* when I knocked was faint. She sat on the leather car seat – the nearest we'd been in all those years – and stared into my face before she spoke. Was she checking for the same wear and tear that I looked for in her? The headscarf – the one she wore while milking – tied her hair back; so I couldn't see how grey she'd become. Her forehead, though, was more lined than I'd expected, the flesh on the side of her face not in shadow wasn't so much pale as waxen, and the flushed red on the back of her hands might've meant a touch of blood pressure. The legs, what was visible of them, were less curved than when she was in the cowhouse, milking Betsy – that's what close-up does. But no matter. Had there been the hint of a smile before she apologized for troubling me? No trouble, I said.

Then down to business. But before that I would sit – of my own choice, seeing as I wasn't asked. To keep facing Kate, I sat in the soot corner. Would've been nice to have replaced old Pat there; me and her across the fire from each other every night. We'd listen to Michael Dillon and the half-six news and, after *Farmers' Forum* at ten o'clock of a Wednesday night, climb those stairs together. At least one of our grown-up family might've taken to the music, while the others would dance a set there on the flagstone – still hadn't cracked either: a good day's work, that. But dreams of might've-beens don't last long. Too many spectres.

It felt strange being there: as if the kitchen were full of gauze curtains, flimsy as gossamer in late September, almost visible. A whole passageway of mist-like curtains seemed to hang from a level above the ceiling. And all I had to do was move them aside, one at a time, to see more clearly the faces of those long gone. Spooks. First it was Nanny's, and Pat's was behind another; then that of my mother. None of them appeared to be either sad or smiling – and I wanted to know. My brother, Mylie, laughed, though I couldn't understand why: he'd had such a hard going when the consumption eventually over-took him. From behind the very last curtain, Philly appeared: black holes for eyes, with dark rings round them. Gradually, stark eyes materialized in his sockets and stared into space over my shoulder. He lowered the eyes.

Stop looking at me – looking through me. Stop blaming me, you bastard – *tochas ar do ghabhal*. Of course I married her; you weren't around. Left her with a fine bundle though, didn't you, before you fecked off? You had choices; I had none – somebody had to have pity on her. Who else would've given them a home? I gave the boy a name. Kept the bail-chain round my neck down the years, to ensure your seed got nurtured. And now look at your line.

I've paid my debt. So fuck off, stop blaming me. I no longer need castigating eyes upon me, or your eerie space to walk in. So, away with you now, spook. And shag off, the lot of you.

To business. Kate said she wanted to leave the farm and property to Simon. Hardly surprising, since she too knew he was Philly's offspring – was there anyone left in these parts who didn't know? Yet it sounded distasteful, even coarse, to have his real identity brought up and his future discussed in such a matter-of-fact way, a bit too bare-faced for taste.

Would I have any objection if she were to ask him to come back from England and take up farming? What say had I in the matter, or what difference would it make if I did object? Maybe I had regrets, a foreboding of the disruption it might cause. But I had no objections. Why would I have?

I felt a peculiar distance to the sound of her voice; as though she were talking from another room, or down a barrel – *at* you instead of *to* you. As if what she had to say was no big deal. That the past was what mattered: those significant things still there on the dresser. The Zam-buk in the green tin that Philly had prised open to rub on the base of his thumb, the box of Rinso and a Kerry Maid round tin where the tea was kept were more immediate than her words. And as for her proposal of Simon's return: it just didn't seem that important. I might as well've been outside the glass gawking in.

Look, girl, the magic is in the past – there is nothing else – and the past is back, if only for a moment. Can't you see it? Listen, hear the lingering reel, St Anne's Reel. Night after night, me there near you – were you not aware of it? I thought you saw them too, heard their magic and longed for a return of the old days.

But the woman couldn't read my thoughts or tune in to my wavelength – we'd never before managed that. Anyway, we expected too much of each other. Our world was full of shagging expectations. For twenty years we waited for the future, and the next thirty were a mix-up. But from fifty on, all we can do is harp back to the old days. So maybe the woman was right to've had nothing on her mind but the future. What fecking future, though, when all there is is gone? When it was here, the past went by like a train down the line. And thinking of trains . . .

Did you have a pleasant trip? I ask Simon. And he catches my hand in both of his: a good firm clasp. He introduces his wife, Nora, and his two offspring.

There's something about them. Can't quite put my finger on it. A certain ingredient: an understanding – without the expectation – between them, maybe. A bond of some kind. Those two youngsters would put hope back in an old fellow's breast. When they smile, I feel the lifting of an ancient pall, the way a bad night's fog gets burned off by the early sun. A certain lightness.

Or as old Marty Nolan used to put it: Like you can see for ever from the top of the Blackstairs, of a clear day in September.

TWENTY-ONE

In the few months since they came home, Simon and his clan have knitted in well. It's like they were always here. They've brought new life to Kellys' above. Talk about energy! They're forever looking for things to do and places to go. The lug seems to be non-stop carting them around – something to keep his nose out of other people's business. I get plagued regularly by Simon to go with them: for the spin, like as if I'd never been outside my own door.

Today, we went to a match in Kilkenny. It was a bit cramped, though, in the back of the Ford; had to prop myself between the mudguard and the spars. I think it's the same make of old van the fish-jowlters out of town come round in, of a Wednesday in the fall of the year – smells like it, too. *Fresh herrings, fresh herrings!* They're not herrings; they're blooming pilchards. Catch the fin and see.

The driver wasn't the best. On the way back, he jumped the queue, a half-mile of cars stopped at the level crossing, and drove right up to the barrier. Will you for feck's sake slow down, I ordered him. But the clown did it on purpose. Every time we went into a bend, I expected to meet my Maker on the other side, coming out. Even the young fellow, Bob, went pale round the gills once or twice. A grand young fellow, though. Be the hokey, he reminds me of a lad I knew a long time ago, and I think he likes the music. He has jet-black curly hair.

They thought I didn't notice their smirks and glances, but it suited me to keep a straight face and let them have their fun at my expense: kept them amused. What they didn't know was that I've taken to going along with them. Being rolled from side to side in the back of a van beats having too much of your own company of a Sunday.

I wasn't that uncomfortable in the back. The shocking-red leather car seat – got to sit on that thing, at last – not fixed to the floor, had been donated like a bag of rags to a jumble sale. We were ready for take-off outside Kellys' the first Sunday I went with them, when this knock came to the back of the van and the door opened. Kate in her blue bib, the one with red flowers and a red border, stood looking in; the car seat on the ground beside her.

Why don't you take this? says she. A sublime

moment, and a thousand years of ice melted there and then.

Comfortable enough too, it is, when the driver's not tumbling us round bends. The three boys, with the little fellow in the middle, sat up front facing the world coming at us. Cha started to lilt, and before long the others joined in. Lilting and rolling the whole road to Kilkenny.

Of course when we got there, I didn't go to the hurling pitch. Can never bring myself to watch a match. Their account of it later on the road home is what I liked. The story is the thing. And to see the mesmerized look on the healthy red cheeks of that young lad, Bob.

Yous go on, I says, while I mind the van. Leave the key, I might take a stroll. As soon as they'd gone into the match, I got out and stretched my legs for an hour along the road outside Kilkenny. Nothing to beat a good walk for keeping a hold of the mind.

While we were at the match, Nora and the young one, May, would've crossed Kellys' yard, walked down the road, over the bridge and up the lane. The cottage door open, they'd have gone in without knocking, to be met by the smell of freshly baked currant bread – and a strong whiff of smoke. After tea, my wife no doubt went upstairs for her old shoeboxes, untied the knots and laid out her stash of photos, letters and mementos across the brand new oilcloth table cover – it's brown this time, the colour of her eyes. And that Maysie of old would've come to life to enthrall them for the afternoon. I can almost hear the laughter in the kitchen. Oh, don't you know the carry-on.

It's getting dark as we get back to Kellys' – now Byrnes', I suppose. They rush inside to have their supper, while I take my time getting out and removing the red seat to bring it in and fix it back on the timber frame over by the fanners.

Instead of crossing the yard to go home after leaving the kitchen, I go over to sit on the window sill for a little while. It happens automatically, a ritual, and by way of composing myself. Don't old habits die hard?

Anyway, I'd rather be out here looking in than on the inside, ill at ease and not knowing what to say. This is where I belong. I still come here from time to time to check. To look through the glass at the new household – that fresh cycle of life – without the craving to be close to it. Without any great impulse. It's good to watch new faces, and their frenzy of events, mingle with the old spectres and the world of the bygone – who've maybe lost some of their hold over me. Hope it grigs them old tormentors that they no longer drive me demented.

Then after supper, the new man inside strikes up the accordion, and his wife, his two children and his aunt, on cue, bluster onto the floor and flicker their feet to the reel. It's heel to toe, on that special flagstone there, as piercing as soldiers' bayonets. The timing, yet easy rhythm, of the small boy's movements is identical to that of one who was once a friend of mine. He's got the gift of the secret language, all right, that only music people understand. A foregathering of old ghosts emerges from the shadows to crowd round, crook their heads and gawp in amazement. Not so much a balance between two worlds, it is more like a change of guard. A continuation of things.

Neah, ded diddley a, diddley aten naten yaa,
Da ded diddley a, diddley aten naten naa . . .

Time to leave them at it. I have a home to go to, to rest this bag of bones. Out the gate, down the road and once more into the dark. Though the nights are not what they used to be: all this electric light nowadays.

Across the land, yard lamps and bulbs hanging from ceilings glow through glass, and dot the expanse. Slick beams from the headlamps of cars cut up and down mountain lanes, and shine all across the valley of Achadhbheatha. They carry the business of daytime into nighttime. And there's an afterglow in the sky that meddles with the crisp sparkle from the stars over Aillenafaha hill. The border between day and night is less definite.

Hunters of the dark, as well as old spectres, are losing part of their domain. Badgers, foxes and owls leave it till late to go on the prowl, or risk getting caught in the light. My accomplices' realm is being pushed back farther into the woods. Creatures of the sun had better watch out or they'll make our kind extinct. We might even lose our feel for the kill. Then there'll be no night scavengers left to clear away the shreds of daytime.

Still 'n' all, nowadays, I'm developing different instincts, and I have other expectations. And they're beginning to rise. So away we go. All together now – one two three.

Neah, ded diddley a . . .

THE END